"I GUESS WE'RE STILL AT WAR,"
SHE SAID QUIETLY.

Nick didn't answer.

"I almost didn't show up."

"Oh, I was sure you'd decide it was worth it to hang in." He gave her a long, hard look.

"What does that mean?" Annie retorted.

"You're smart. Figure it out."

Annie knew she was getting nowhere fast. "How does your ankle feel?" She tried to keep the edge out of her voice.

"Your concern is touching, Doc."

"And your sarcasm is infuriating. Could we take a walk and talk in private about what's going on?"

"I'm not walking very well these days, and I don't much feel like chatting. Why don't we accept the reality of the situation? You do your job and I'll do mine. If we play our cards right, we'll both come out ahead."

"And I accused you of being adolescent! You're absolutely infantile, Nick Winters! And if you want to behave like a child, I'll start treating you as one."

A CANDLELIGHT ECSTASY SUPREME

1 TEMPESTUOUS EDEN, *Heather Graham*
2 EMERALD FIRE, *Barbara Andrews*
3 WARMED BY THE FIRE, *Donna Kimel Vitek*
4 LOVERS AND PRETENDERS, *Prudence Martin*
5 TENDERNESS AT TWILIGHT, *Megan Lane*
6 TIME OF A WINTER LOVE, *Jo Calloway*
7 WHISPER ON THE WIND, *Nell Kincaid*
8 HANDLE WITH CARE, *Betty Jackson*
9 NEVER LOOK BACK, *Donna Kimel Vitek*
10 NIGHT, SEA, AND STARS, *Heather Graham*
11 POLITICS OF PASSION, *Samantha Hughes*
12 NO STRINGS ATTACHED, *Prudence Martin*
13 BODY AND SOUL, *Anna Hudson*
14 CROSSFIRE, *Eileen Bryan*
15 WHERE THERE'S SMOKE . . . , *Nell Kincaid*
16 PAYMENT IN FULL, *Jackie Black*
17 RED MIDNIGHT, *Heather Graham*
18 A HEART DIVIDED, *Ginger Chambers*
19 SHADOW GAMES, *Elise Randolph*
20 JUST HIS TOUCH, *Emily Elliott*
21 BREAKING THE RULES, *Donna Kimel Vitek*
22 ALL IN GOOD TIME, *Samantha Scott*
23 SHADY BUSINESS, *Barbara Andrews*
24 SOMEWHERE IN THE STARS, *Jo Calloway*
25 AGAINST ALL ODDS, *Eileen Bryan*
26 SUSPICION AND SEDUCTION, *Shirley Hart*
27 PRIVATE SCREENINGS, *Lori Herter*
28 FASCINATION, *Jackie Black*
29 DIAMONDS IN THE SKY, *Samantha Hughes*
30 EVENTIDE, *Margaret Dobson*
31 CAUTION: MAN AT WORK, *Linda Randall Wisdom*
32 WHILE THE FIRE RAGES, *Amii Lorin*

PLAYING IT SAFE

Alison Tyler

7H 84

A CANDLELIGHT ECSTASY SUPREME

Published by
Dell Publishing Co., Inc.
1 Dag Hammarskjold Plaza
New York, New York 10017

For Rebecca, David, and Jeff—the best cheering squad a writer could have.

Dell ® TM 681510, Dell Publishing Co., Inc.

Candlelight Ecstasy Supreme is a trademark of Dell Publishing Co., Inc.

Candlelight Ecstasy Romance®, 1,203,540, is a registered trademark of Dell Publishing Co., Inc.

ISBN: 0–440–16944–5

Printed in the United States of America
First printing—July 1984

To Our Readers—

Candlelight Ecstasy is delighted to announce the start of a brand-new series—Ecstasy Supremes! Now you can enjoy a romance series unlike all the others—longer and more exciting, filled with more passion, adventure, and intrigue—the stories you've been waiting for.

In months to come we look forward to presenting books by many of your favorite authors and the very finest work from new authors of romantic fiction as well. As always, we are striving to present the unique, absorbing love stories that you enjoy most—the very best love has to offer.

Breathtaking and unforgettable, Ecstasy Supremes will follow in the great romantic tradition you've come to expect *only* from Candlelight Ecstasy.

Your suggestions and comments are always welcome. Please let us hear from you.

Sincerely,

The Editors
Candlelight Romances
1 Dag Hammarskjold Plaza
New York, New York 10017

PROLOGUE

Coiling in readiness, Nick Winters bent low for the Aussie's dipping volley. The ball exploded off his tennis racket with tremendous topspin, causing Willie Norrison, Australia's new young hopeful, to hesitate in confusion for that one fatal moment. Nick Winters always kept his opponent guessing. Today all of his artillery was out; his precision, his confident sense of authority, power, and finesse were displayed in regal form. Norrison had the advantage of youth, but Winters was used to wiping the courts with overeager young men like his increasingly nervous opponent.

Nicholas Winters was the undisputed superstar of professional tennis, having held reign for nearly fifteen years—astounding in a sport where youth was always on the ready to step in and take over the limelight, to put the older players in their place. No one could touch Winters. He was a brilliant master in the art of tennis with a style and form no other player could match. He was also irascible, hot tempered, dramatically emotional, and utterly outrageous on the courts. To top it off, he was remarkable looking, with brooding gray eyes, a shock of wild black curly hair, a thick mustache which gave his face a rough, yet sensuous, image, and a lean, athletic body that showed proudly the effect of exercise and good fortune.

In the second set the crowd sat back waiting for Winters to walk off with an easy, surefire win. Only, something started going wrong. Winters had just turned full circle to the baseline for a disguised lob that had sailed over his head. He missed it. The crowd clearly overheard his angry self-reproach. Then, when a linesman made a call against Winters in the crucial seventh game of the second set, Winters became incensed, arguing that the ball was inside the line by a mile. The crowd seemed to agree, supporting his anger with some cheers and applause. The linesman held to his decision, the umpire refusing to reverse it. Winters seemed about to blow up, but then at the last minute pulled in the reins. Norrison took the second set. Winters stared sullenly at his tennis racket, twirling it idly about in his hands.

Winters seemed to rally in the third set, getting a second wind with each succeeding game. He ended up turning the final set into a slashing, exciting encounter. Out there fighting, he moved to net to keep on the offense. This was the kind of match the crowd adored.

In that last winning swing, Winters leaped up, both feet off the ground, to return the ball with a crackling forehand. Everyone in the stadium cheered. It had turned out to be a great match, a Winters special.

The crowd, busy clapping and gathering their things together, failed to notice the contorted pain on Winters's face as he turned from the net. But one person saw the raw anguish reflected in his features as he approached the rim of the amphitheater. Nick Winters glanced up mindlessly to the emptying stands. His eyes met hers in shocked surprise, driving the pained, tense grimace from his face. The woman gazed down at him, motionless. Her face offered no clue to what she was feeling.

CHAPTER ONE

Annie Kneeland shifted her silver BMW sedan down to first gear as she swung into the parking lot. The intense Florida sun made her squint despite her sunglasses. For a moment she didn't see the car neatly tucked into her reserved parking spot. She stepped hard on the brakes. The jolt went right through her, but it had far less to do with the abrupt stop than with her recognition of the car occupying her space.

For a long moment Annie sat in her car, her hands gripping the wheel. Finally she forced herself to move. It took all the calm she could muster to guide her sedan into another spot. Once that had been accomplished, she again felt the same immobility.

Why had he come? Yet even as she asked herself the question, she knew the answer; she had known he would show up. From the moment he'd spotted her up in the stands three days ago, she'd been waiting for this confrontation. But it didn't lessen the shock or the mounting tension.

When she'd gone to the Delray Beach tennis tournament three days ago, she had almost convinced herself that she was only going for the women's doubles match. But she knew the whole time she'd sat through the women's games that she would stay for the men's semifinals. It was a foolish test. She was going to prove to herself that Nick Winters no longer mattered. But she was too smart to convince herself that was the reason. The truth was she felt compelled to see him again and she thought it would be a safe way to do so. Only it hadn't worked out that way. The moment he'd spotted her in the stands, a lot of things came into focus for Annie. Ten months had not been nearly enough time apart to undo any of her feelings about this man —not her attraction, her anger, or her pain. To add to that, she was furious at herself for having been fool enough to go to the tennis tournament in the first place.

Now that she was about to face Nick once more, Annie focused in on the most important fact—she was never going to allow Nick Winters to gain the edge again. She stepped out of her car, looked over at Nick's sleek black Porsche and then at the sign posted in front of it: DR. ANN KNEELAND printed in bold black lettering. She calmed down a little. After all, this was her territory and Nick's usurping of her parking spot was not going to usurp her authority or control. Armed with that reminder she strode across the lot toward the Fisher Sports Medicine Center.

The center was one of those low, modern buildings that exuded style and high-tech class. The side facing the parking lot was white-washed stone with very few windows. Large skylights illuminated the waiting room. The doctors' suites all faced the rear of the building and each of these had a full wall of glass that looked out onto the Atlantic Ocean. On the lower level the physical therapy rooms also opened to the water. It was a beautiful building in a beautiful setting—one of the choicest spots in Delray Beach.

Today as she stepped into the waiting room she was oblivious to the striking architecture, the luxurious appointments, even the stunning contrast of temperatures. The building might be a good thirty degrees cooler, but Annie's temper hadn't dropped a fraction. Her angry eyes scanned the room, ready to do battle with Nick. She was determined to keep her edge right from the start.

The waiting room was empty except for Paula Jackson, who was busy opening the morning mail behind her desk. It was only nine A.M. None of the other four doctors at the Center scheduled appointments before ten. Two of the physicians were out of town at a conference and Cal Wheeler spent Monday mornings at the hospital. Annie had spotted Doug Fisher's Mercedes in the parking lot. He often came in early to catch up on administrative business. Annie doubted that the esteemed head of the Center would be too happy with her lambasting one of the biggest sports figures around today. She was sure he'd like nothing better than to add Nick's name to his list of patients. But Annie knew

Nick's presence had nothing to do with seeking medical help.

She shrugged off Doug's likely reactions, deciding she might as well add insult to injury. Doug was none too happy with her these days anyway. He had barely been civil since she'd handed in her resignation three weeks ago. When Annie told him she was accepting an offer from St. Mead's Children's Hospital in New York City to cohead their orthopedic clinic, Doug had taken it as a personal affront. He could not understand why any physician in her right mind would trade a place in one of the most prosperous, elite clinics in the country to work in some poor, rundown hospital in the slums of New York. Annie didn't bother trying to explain. Physicians like Doug Fisher had a tendency to be far more interested in the establishment of their elite reputations and in the achievement of acclaim than in the more nitty-gritty business of medicine.

With a puzzled frown Annie asked Paula, "Where is *he*?"

"And a cheery good-morning to you, too." Paula grinned. "And if you are referring to the incredible Nick Winters, he's waiting for you in your office. You never told me the two of you were old friends."

"We're not," Annie growled. "We just go back a long way." She was stretching the truth. Years ago they had been friends. They had grown up together and there had been a time in her adolescence when Annie had believed Nick was her best friend. And of course much more recently she had thought they were a lot more than friends. It was easier to think of the long-ago past than it was to dwell on her more recent and far more devastating relationship with Nick.

Paula, concerned by Annie's odd expression, said, "I hope it was okay to let him in, Annie."

Annie gave Paula a strained nod. It wasn't really okay, but that had nothing to do with Paula. Why did he have to show up now, causing those wounds to open again when she'd thought they had finally begun to heal? And why did she have to be the one who had instigated the whole thing? Ten months ago, when she'd told Nick she never wanted to see him again, she had really believed she meant it. But knowing he was in town this week, so close after all this time, something had driven her to take one final look. It wasn't final at all.

Annie threw open the door to her office. Nick Winters was casually sitting half-reclined in her swivel chair as she stepped inside. In that brief walk down the hall she had steeled herself to face him with controlled calm. But seeing him made any hope disappear that she would keep her cool.

"What the hell are you doing here?" Her voice quivered as she spoke.

"Is that any way for a physician to greet an ailing patient? Where's your bedside manner gone, Doc?" Nick Winters sat forward in the chair and blatantly surveyed her, his dark, almost black eyes traveling slowly from her head to her toes. His sensual smile was even more infuriating than his survey. She was also quick to realize that by sitting in her chair and forcing her to stand before him, Nick had put her at an awkward and extremely uncomfortable disadvantage. She hadn't forgotten how talented he was at doing that.

Taking firm strides, Annie walked over to the desk. She concentrated on regaining her composure, determined not to let Nick maintain the advantage.

"If you have come to see me as a patient, then please go back into the waiting room and make an appointment," she said in her most professional tone. "And please get out of my chair." That last remark unfortunately sounded petulant, and Annie tried to ignore Nick's grinning response.

"Of course, Doc." He stood up immediately, stepped aside, and with a grand, sweeping gesture motioned her to her seat. "The throne is all yours," he quipped as he stepped back around the desk and slid his lanky body into a chair facing her.

"Your attractive nurse already told me I could see you now, since it is an emergency. But I promise," he said, lifting his hand up in a boy scout salute, "to make specific appointments in the future. I certainly wouldn't want to have my doctor continue to feel so uptight. You might jab a needle into me in the wrong place."

"Believe me," Annie said, a flicker of amusement curling her lips, "the idea is extremely appealing."

"You still look terrific when you're mad." He grinned.

"You should know," she threw back. "You've seen me that way more than most."

"That's true. We did have some rousing fights when we were kids." Nick rested his hands complacently on his lean, hard stomach. He was not feeling nearly as cool as he appeared. It had been almost a year since their last encounter. Seeing her the other day had thrown him for a loop. And given him a flicker of hope.

"I wasn't referring to childhood battles." Their last fight on that hot summer night ten months ago was still so vivid in Annie's mind she could have recited the words by heart.

"You're still so mad."

He said it in such a way that Annie couldn't tell if it was a question or a statement.

Nick wasn't sure, either. He had been shaken right down to his tennis sneakers the other day seeing her in the stands. He had thought she'd meant it, too, when she'd told him she never wanted to see him again. Then, like some kind of a miracle, she turns up after all this time looking even better than the fantasies that had haunted him. Dark, ruby-colored hair that shimmered with a radiant health as it flowed in gentle waves to her shoulders, strikingly defined features that still managed to evoke warmth for all their chiseled fineness, and eyes the color of a tropical aquamarine ocean, large as saucers, seething at him now with barely controlled rage. For a moment he forgot that seeing her again was not the only reason he had come here. Remembering, he felt his stomach twist into an all-too-familiar knot. It was a psychological reaction to his mounting concern. Strung tighter than he'd even admit to himself, he'd felt the tension increasing steadily over the past few months. It was beginning to tear him apart and he was banking on Annie to have a solution.

"I was surprised to see you at my match the other day. Last I remembered you swore you'd never come within a thousand miles of me. You added a few choice words to that, I believe." He intentionally kept the words light, pushing his deeper feelings aside. Maybe she'd had justification in breaking off their relationship, but it didn't alter his inner anguish or his longing. He had been determined to keep away, but he had begun slipping as soon as he'd come into town for the World Tennis Championship tournament. He'd got as far as dialing her number several times, but never made it through to a ring. She had told him it was over and Nick was usually not the kind of man who went around banging his head against stone walls. Her showing up the other day had changed everything.

"You've got a good memory, Nick. And I thought you weren't even listening. Have you shown up almost a year later to gloat over proving me wrong?"

"Still ready for a fight," he said, grinning. "Some things don't change."

"How true. You certainly haven't. Still the old Wild Man. Tell me, doesn't it ever get tiring after all these years to stand out there having infantile temper tantrums? Then again, I guess your fans wouldn't love you any other way."

She slid her chair back an inch. In that same cold voice she said, "I have a lot of work to do, Nick. And I'm not interested in reminiscing about old times." She could feel the tightness in her throat as she spoke.

"I haven't come here to reminisce, either. I guess I thought after seeing you at the match that we might—"

"Forget what you thought," Annie said bitterly. "I still can't figure out what I was doing there. I do know it wasn't because of any notions I had about starting anything again."

Nick's voice was softly serious as he studied her. "I thought being a doctor and all, you would have learned how to cure old wounds."

She wanted to deny those wounds still existed, but her anger had already given her away. If it still didn't feel so bad, why all the rage? Nick's eyes held that intense, searching gaze that used to go right through her. But not today, she told herself. She was not going to let him get to her now. People are supposed to learn from their experiences, right? Especially rotten experiences. And Nick Winters had provided her with a bird's eye view of a first-class louse at play.

"Last year is over, Nick. I'm working on a new one. And I don't really care to discuss it further.

Besides, we already had that discussion almost a year ago."

"If I recall, you did all the 'discussing' that time. You hardly gave me a chance to get a word in edgewise."

He recalled a lot of things—like meeting her again after eight years. At first when he'd spotted her at the wedding of a mutual friend a year and a half ago, he had felt awkward and uncomfortable. Eight years back, they had not parted on the best of terms.

Annie had entered the pro tennis circuit when she was sixteen, mostly due to Nick's support and encouragement. They were close friends in those days, but it was also a time in Nick's life when he was flying high, completely caught up in the stardom and glamor of his success as a tennis player. He was so caught up in his own fast-moving world that he completely forgot about his date with Annie after her high school graduation. When he had called to apologize she had hung up on him. He wrote her a few times when she was in college, but she never answered his letters. Then as he became more absorbed in his ever-thriving tennis career, he had pushed his guilt aside. But he had never forgotten that Annie was special and that he had messed up a good friendship.

He remembered that Annie had seemed as uncomfortable as he was at the wedding where they'd next met. But they had decided to go for a drink the next day, both seemingly determined to handle the encounter in an adult fashion. That's how it had begun. Their past relationship had provided the bridge, but it hadn't taken long for either of them to discover that something fresh and exciting was happening. They were able to relate on a totally different and more mature level. Everything seemed to click for them. During the six months they were together their relationship flourished, despite Nick's crazy schedule and all the forced times apart. And then it had all crumpled.

Nick shook his head free of that painful time. "Seeing you wasn't the only reason I came here today. I'm having a—a medical problem and I—"

"Oh, come on, Nick. I expected a better ploy than that, even for you."

"Do you think this is easy for me?" Nick growled. "Sure, I wanted to see you again. I even hoped for a minute there that we could still work things out. But obviously you haven't any interest in . . . Look, I am having a problem and I don't like doctors in general." He managed a smile in spite of his anger. "Right now I'm not liking you too much, either. But I do trust you. And I—I value your opinion. Okay, so I might not have ever dared darken your door again if you hadn't reappeared, but when I decided to come here today, it was partly because I am hurting." In more ways than one, he said to himself, but to Annie he simply said, "Will you check me out?" As he talked he found himself having trouble looking at her. This was more difficult than he'd imagined.

Annie was aware of Nick's difficulty and she also knew whatever was bothering him had to be serious. His manner was different, the light banter and even the anger vanishing, his face mirroring the inner tension he was feeling. She was struck by the memory of that same look on his face after that recent tennis match.

Leaning against her desk, Annie said, "Nick. I'm leaving here in a week—permanantly. I'm taking a nice long vacation and then I'm heading for a job in New York. If something is wrong I think you should see Dr. Fisher. He's the best there is." Her angry tone faded, her voice registering concern.

"I want you."

His words had a disquieting affect on her composure. She told herself that he was merely referring to wanting her to treat him, but she couldn't deny the sensual overtones. She was even more emphatic as she answered.

"I can't treat you, Nick. It wouldn't be right. If you needed prolonged care I simply couldn't follow up. Even if I weren't leaving, I couldn't work with you." She backed away, started toward her seat, and then ended up standing by the window. "I'll ask Fisher to see you tomorrow."

Nick got up and walked over to her. "Listen, Annie. It wasn't easy to come here. Let's keep things professional, if that will be easier for you. I'm usually great at ignoring pain. Any athlete, as you know, goes through agonies of the body and spirit if he wants to play the game. It's something you teach yourself to ignore. Well, I've reached a point where denial just isn't working. The pain is beginning to affect my game—badly. You can't have forgotten the pressures, the grind. You were a part of it all."

"And I also left it. Maybe your body is telling you it's time to hang up the racket. You've been swinging that thing since you were eleven years old. I thought last year . . ." No, she reminded herself. I'm not going to talk about last year. I'm not going to remind Nick of all the times we talked until the early hours of the morning about his ambivalence about staying with tennis. It had meant nothing, just like everything else that had gone on between them. His next words acted as confirmation.

"I'm not ready to throw in the towel. In four months I'm going to get my chance to regain my title at Wimbledon. Then hold on to it at the Open. Afterwards if my body gives out—well, I'll deal with that then. Now all I want is to be in top shape to play out the season. Will you at least check me out and offer an opinion?" Nick's gaze remained fastened on her as he spoke. He had gotten through the toughest part. Now he needed the right answer.

She gave it to him.

"I'm only going to do this as a one-shot exam. If you do need follow-up, you will have to see someone else. Where's the pain?"

Annie decided if he smiled victoriously she'd tell him to go show his wounds elsewhere. His face only reflected relief.

"Both my ankles have seen better days, but the left one is causing the most difficulty."

"Okay, hop up on the table and I'll take a look."

Her medical eye quickly observed that he favored the left foot as he walked across the room.

"Do I strip bare or just drop my pants?" He attempted a seductive grin. It didn't quite come off. Annie knew he was scared. She also knew he hated having those feelings and, even more, hated anyone else knowing about it. This was taking a lot of courage on his part. He was obviously hurting far more than he was letting on.

"Just take off your shoes and socks and roll up your slacks. That is—if it's only your ankle that's causing the discomfort."

He threw her a bemused look. Did she sense what kind of effect she still had on him or was she simply being a thorough doctor? Her voice didn't let on.

"Just the ankle, Doc," he answered, not making any effort to conceal his smile.

His ankle had been expertly wrapped with an Ace bandage. "Whose handiwork?" she asked as she carefully unwound it.

"Bill Kenny, one of the trainers. He probably spends half his days coiling them around tennis players' limbs."

"What does he say about your problem?" She tossed the bandage to the side and gently began to feel the ankle. It was quite swollen.

"What he says doesn't really count, Annie. You know that."

Annie understood all too well. Pro tennis was a big-money sport and the star players had a lot riding on them. Promotors expected them to do their thing out on the courts, pain or no pain. The trainers had to get the athletes in shape to get out there and play. They were not about to tell someone as successful as Nick Winters that he shouldn't be running around a court. Besides the pressure from tournament promotors, there were the management firms that regarded the superstars as very valuable property. Few were as valuable as Nick. He was not only a charismatic star of a sport that had skyrocketed over the past ten years to astounding popularity, but he was also extremely good looking in that raw masculine way that made every product he endorsed terrifically appealing simply because he said they were.

The pressure was there from all sides. No wonder Nick wanted an honest, unbiased medical opinion.

"You've got great hands, Doc." He grinned. "Even if your bedside manner could use some ironing out."

The smile vanished as he winced in pain.

"Obviously that hurt," she said, looking up, "despite my great hands. How long exactly have you had this pain?"

"I've lost count how many times I've twisted or sprained my ankles. But I guess this one really started giving me grief eight or nine months ago." He swung sideways as she lifted his leg flat on the table.

"Eight or nine months! Nick, that's positively asinine to let an injury go untended for so long."

"You never did pull any punches. I'm afraid that's going to mean another demerit for bedside manner, Doc."

"Shut up," she snapped, focusing all of her attention on his ankle. "I suppose it never dawned on you to stay off your feet for a couple of months when you get bashed. Your public, no doubt, would be too disappointed if you missed a few tournaments. You do provide that added excitement when you have your little tantrums."

"You're building up those demerits mighty fast. How about some loving sympathy?" he said, smiling. "You used to be a lot sweeter."

"And a lot more naive. Anyway, medical insurance only covers exams, not TLC. I'm sure if that's what you're looking for, there's no end to the women who would line up to accommodate you." She was walking right into it and yet she couldn't seem to keep her mouth shut. Not to mention having trouble keeping her heart from pounding. He could still get to her and Annie didn't like it one bit.

Nick took hold of her hand as she reached toward the X-ray machine.

"How about having dinner tonight?" he asked, taking her more off guard.

She gave him a weary sigh. "We're keeping this professional, remember. I don't have dinner with my patients—or my ex-lovers," she added, determined to spell things out so that neither of them misread the situation. "Now, keep still. I'm going to take some X rays and then I'll be able to assess the damage." She tried her best to steady her pulse and get on with the exam. Thankfully, Nick obeyed for once.

After she took the X rays, Paula carried them off for developing. Annie finished checking Nick out, her suspicions growing more certain as she continued to press and prod. The returned X rays bore out her assumption. It didn't make her happy to have guessed so accurately.

For a few minutes she stared silently at the illuminated skeletal negative. Nick, having returned to the seat opposite her desk, watched her, the knot in his stomach tugging furiously away at his insides. "That bad?"

"I don't know how you've managed to go out there all these months." Using a small pointer she tapped it on a thick white line on the X ray. "This was a fracture, a hairline one, which, had it had time to heal, would have probably mended nicely. But no matter how small the fracture, if you don't attend to it, the bone may not knit back correctly."

"I don't want the details, Annie. Can you do something about it now?" He hadn't meant to sound so harsh.

She ignored his tone. "The best choice— really the only sane one medically—is to operate. So much calcium has form—"

"How much time would it require?" His biting edge was still there, but tempered.

"Nick, the hospital stay would only be a few

28

days. But you would be laid up for two, possibly three months. And I—I couldn't promise you the ankle would be like new again. You've done a real job on it. There are no guarantees someone could undo the damage."

"Between now and Wimbledon I have over sixty matches I'm committed to. An operation is out." He leaned forward in his chair. Annie could see the muscles tensing in his body. "Isn't there anything less drastic you could do to keep me on my feet?"

"In a week? I'm leaving, Nick. Remember? No doctor in this clinic could undo the damage in that amount of time. At the very least someone would have to work with you every day to keep you going. Exercise, medication, at least some prescribed rest. It would mean an ongoing strict regimen. Certainly no sixty matches."

"I can get out of some of them. I'd cancel all but the big ones, the hell with the promotors and hotshot PR creeps."

"Nick, you aren't listening. It would be my last choice. Operating is—"

"Annie, I need these five months. You said yourself, if someone worked with me daily . . ." He let the sentence drop, his mind firmly made up as to who he wanted that someone to be. Could he make her believe it was fate that he had shown up just when she was going to be killing a few months before starting a new job? "Annie, I know you're offering me the best medical advice. After the U.S. Open I'll have the operation. If surgery doesn't work I'll retire, put my miserable feet up on a couch, and spend the rest of my days—"

"Counting your money?" she offered with a cynical smile.

"Yeah. Counting my money, just like the old king in his countinghouse."

"Did you ever think, Nick, that with all your money you could do something other than count it, or buy fancy cars and palaces, jewels for all your lady friends . . . ?" Damn it, why did she have to keep putting her foot into her mouth? Nick's lady friends were no concern of hers. Hadn't she been reminding herself of that for the last ten months? She could feel her face flush.

Nick's smile was partly taunting, partly sad. "You've been reading too many gossip columns," he said, a sigh of disappointment in his voice. "And you still don't understand. I'm not in tennis for the money. Hell, you know I came into the world with a big enough trust fund never to have to remove that silver spoon from my mouth. Tennis is all I ever wanted. By the time I was twelve I knew I was going to be a champion."

"And is that still so important? Nick Winters, superstar extraordinaire. Do you really still crave all that attention?" she asked him scornfully.

"Even the boos and hisses when I let off steam out there. You've got it, babe, I eat it up. So did you for a while." He strode over to where she stood. He was angry and feeling defensive. And damned if he was going to tell her that he was scared that without tennis there would be nothing else. He'd be nothing else. Money bought a person a lot of things, but it didn't buy an identity.

"I discovered I wanted more out of life than stardom," Annie retorted sharply, trying to ignore the heat behind her anger—the heat Nick's presence still generated. In a tight whisper she added, "I grew up."

"I can see," Nick murmured. They were standing so close. He hadn't planned on doing anything. Certainly Annie hadn't. When his arms suddenly reached out for her and she came into them, their lips meeting, it really took them both by surprise. But then, as their kiss deepened, neither of them thought about anything except how good it felt and how long they'd both nurtured fantasies about this moment.

CHAPTER TWO

"You say one word, Nicholas Winters—one snide remark—and I'll go after you with the biggest hypodermic needle I've got."

"Not a word, Doc. Anyway, I'd just as soon kiss you again."

Annie brought her fingers up to her lips, then nervously dropped her hand back down to her side.

"That kiss might have wrought havoc a year ago, Nick, but you've lost your point this time," Annie said sarcastically. The bite was a touch too breathy to have the intended sting. She longed to move back, to edge away from him, but she was still determined not to give him the advantage. Oh, well, one slip. But that kiss had caught her off guard. Now she was prepared. Still, she wished he'd give her some breathing space. He held his ground as determinedly as she held hers.

"Annie, I've thought about you a lot these past—"

"Come on, Nick. Spare me the line, okay? We

just got carried away for the moment. It doesn't change anything."

"You're not going to give me an inch, are you?" Nick drew still closer as he spoke.

"You aren't giving me much room, either," she answered wryly, smiling despite her effort to stay annoyed.

He rested his hands lightly on her shoulders. "No matter what you think, Anna Falanna, I'm telling you the truth."

It was the old nickname he used to tease her with when they were kids, especially when she became impossible. He'd also used it a few choice times only a year ago. Hearing it again brought back too many memories.

"You're still beautiful, Annie. Again—not a line. The truth. Just like it's true that I've missed you and thought about you"—he carefully omitted "and wanted you"—"more often than I should admit. After all, I never like playing defensively."

"Very true. But you get a thrill out of putting everyone else on the defensive." This time she did back off and turn away.

"You were once my best friend, Annie." His words were whisper-soft.

The hint of sadness in his voice made her turn around. She looked at him with hurt surprise. "You had a hell of a way of showing it."

"Annie, I didn't come here today to try to make up for the past or even try to offer excuses. I came because I was—"

"In pain. And you wanted me to perform

33

some magic and make it go away. After all, what are old friends for."

"Stop it, Annie. You're trying so damn hard to be tough. Your kiss told me a lot more than your scornful glares and angry words. You still feel something for me." He came toward her again.

"Nick, why are you doing this? What is the point of this seduction scene?" She kept her voice steady, but she could not mask how troubled she felt.

"Tell me something. What were you feeling the other day when you looked down at me from the stands?" He studied her face intently. Once again their eyes locked.

For several moments she said nothing. Then, taking a sharp breath, she said, "I told you I don't know why I even went. Maybe it was to confirm the whole thing was really over."

"And did you?"

Instead of answering his question, she let her words drift back in time. "When we were kids I adored you, worshiped you. You were my brother, my friend, my—my first love. That night you stood me up I thought my heart would break and that you were the biggest louse I'd ever known." She paused for a moment and smiled, Nick silently watching her.

"A first-class case of infatuation. Time has a way of curing those hurts. When we met again last year I thought you had grown up. Oh, Nick, you can be so damn charming and warm. And so loving and sensitive. All the things I was looking for. What I hadn't bargained on was the

34

same old deceit and game playing. You're almost as good a con artist as you are a tennis player, Nick. For months I bought your story that all those columns about you and Lynn Carey were nothing but trumped up PR. The golden pair of the pro circuit."

"It was true. Most of what they wrote in the papers was pure fiction."

"Even the pending engagement?" She shook her head. "Why am I going through this all again? Nick, don't you see that it wasn't just your deception about Lynn that made me finally see the reality? When I read about your breakup afterward, it didn't matter. I wasn't even surprised. In the end it wasn't any woman who drew us apart. It was your first love, and maybe your only love—tennis. Playing the game is all that really matters to you. And you still won't relax your grip, half-crippled and constantly in pain. For a while there I thought we were heading in the same direction, but we've always wanted different things out of life. Let's consider that kiss just now as a final good-bye." The words came out okay. Now if only she could fully believe them. She always had been a good talker, and this little speech made a lot of sense to her. She even meant it on one level. But her heart always seemed to be the last to get the message.

Nick walked over to the window. Staring out at the ocean, yet not really seeing anything, he said softly, "I need your help. There is no one else I trust. It's funny. Until just now I didn't realize in how many ways you could matter to me." He swung around, his eyes glistening as the sun cast a glow across his features. "Annie, don't you find it strange that I would show up needing you just when you happen to have a few months to spare, months that could mean everything to me?"

"Come on, Nick. I gave up believing in fate at the same time I stopped believing in Santa Claus. There isn't a chance in a million that I would take that on. Haven't you heard anything I've said?"

"Every word. But I have a habit of reading between the lines. Annie, would it really be that awful? Despite what you think, I have changed. I had to learn the hard way that honesty is the best policy. If you want to keep things purely professional I promise to respect your wishes. Besides, it would be a great vacation."

"It wouldn't be a vacation," Annie argued.

"I won't be a bad patient, Doc. I'll follow orders, take my medicine, eat all my spinach . . ."

"You'd be impossible and you know it. You haven't listened to anyone since you were a kid. And I've been the route of pro tours, and it's no picnic. As you pointed out to me, I remember the grind, the pressures, the infighting, the thirst for victory. I don't want any part of it."

"That's not why you're resisting. You're scared you wouldn't stand a chance in hell of keeping our relationship professional." His words cut through her defense.

"If your ego needs some bolstering, you can relax. You haven't lost your sensual appeal. Sure, that's a part of it—a small part." She was lying through her teeth. It was the biggest part of all. He still had that same magnetic appeal. Only she kept reminding herself she was older and wiser. She had finally learned how to look after her own best interests and Nick Winters was most definitely *not* one of them. "Anyway, separate from having no interest in another empty affair with you, I happen to have a job waiting for me on August first at St. Mead's. It's a little hospital on the Lower East Side of New York. Quite a change from the gloss and glamor of my life here. I'll be running a new children's orthopedic unit. The work is going to require every ounce of energy and time I have. Between now and August I am going to take the first real break I've given myself since medical school. Following you around the world is the last thing I need."

"And the thing I need the most. You could get me through these next few months, Annie. If I promise to behave would it make any difference? No strain, no demands, no seductions."

"Nick, what's more to the point is that I don't even think you should finish out this season. If you were really willing to follow my orders you'd check yourself into a hospital."

"I already told you that was out. Why don't we just forget the whole thing?" A frosty mask came over Nick's face. He didn't beg. With or without Annie Kneeland he was going to make it. He had to. There was no way Nick Winters was going to crawl out of pro tennis, not after he had soared to the greatest heights the profession offered. No. He'd put in too damn much of himself to have it end like that. He wished he hadn't come to see her. He was angry that she had turned down his not-so-silent cry for help. But worse, now he knew he would never get her out of his mind—or heart.

Annie almost gave in. He was hurting and she wanted to reach out and soothe him. She wanted to be there for him, help him. But she would have to pay a heavy price. Nick was right. She didn't stand a chance of keeping their involvement professional. She had been honest with him when she'd said she didn't want a brief affair. She had already gotten a taste of that last year. Of course she hadn't known then it would lead to nothing. Now she was painfully versed in Nick's manipulations and deceptions. He was still wed to tennis, still playing all the games off court, too, that went with being a big-name star. Annie had gotten through the initial stages of loss. She had finished shedding her tears. There was a new sense of direction and purpose in her life and Nick Winters wasn't going to mess with it. Working with poor kids at St. Mead's was exactly what she wanted. So why was she having such a hard time sticking to her guns?

Paula buzzed her.

"Hank Luther is here for his appointment."

"I'll be with him in a minute, Paula. Could you get him set up, please?"

"Will do."

Nick smiled. "Hank Luther? Football player. Very impressive, Doctor. You've done well."

"Better than I'd have fared in tennis, anyway." She smiled back.

"You never did have the hunger for it," he said quietly.

"No, I never did."

He had to leave. Yet it wasn't easy to turn around and walk out the door. He lingered awkwardly, wishing somehow he could make things different. Only he knew he couldn't. And shouldn't. Annie was right. They were enmeshed in two different worlds and he had no right to ask her to traipse around the globe with him, administering to his hurts. Even if she was, very likely, the only one who could. And he wasn't thinking merely about his ankle. Annie had always understood him, recognized the part of him that was fragile. He had no doubt she could see his vulnerability now. It didn't matter.

As he turned to go, Annie said, "Take care of yourself, Nick."

He smiled, paused, then walked back over to her.

Could a kiss physically hurt? The gentle, brief touch of his lips on hers stirred an aching pain that made Annie wince, catching her breath speechlessly. It's just as well, she told herself with a sigh as the door shut, taking Nick out of her life again. I might have said something I'd live to regret.

* * *

Boxes were stacked everywhere. Annie's apartment looked very much like a large warehouse preparing for a major rummage sale. In a couple of days the furniture and some of the cartons would be going into storage, because until she found an apartment in New York City she had no place else to put everything.

"How did I ever manage to collect so much junk?" Annie stared bleakly around the living room. The clutter made the large open area feel closed in. It matched her mood.

"It's not so bad," Paula said comfortingly. "Anyway, I'm going to help myself to a lot of it."

"Are you sure you want this stuff, or are you just taking pity on me?" Annie pulled open one of the boxes.

"For instance, here we have at least two dozen totally pointless kitchen gadgets, most of which I never figured out the use for. And over here"—she laughed, digging out a somewhat lopsided clay vase—"is a very valuable objet d'art that no one should be without."

Paula grinned. "Listen, that beauty is earmarked for my mother-in-law's Christmas present. It's the perfect item to repay her for that godawful chartreuse chipper dipper she sent me last year." They both laughed, Paula adding, "I have to admit you are an unbelievable packrat, Annie."

"I know. Every so often something comes over me. I'll be walking by a shop, see some utterly ridiculous item, decide I really might need it sometime, and then shove it into another drawer or stick it on a shelf—for safekeeping. Then there are all the things people give me. Some of my patients have come up with a few winners. But, I never can get myself to throw anything out."

"Well, then, this is good therapy. By moving a thousand miles away you've got to let go of all the old stuff you've been holding on to."

Annie had a funny expression on her face again. Like yesterday, when Paula had told her about her surprise visitor. After Nick Winters left—Paula had recognized him immediately— Annie had walked around half in a fog for the rest of the day.

Curious, but not wanting to pry, Paula asked lightly, "Want to talk about it?"

"Letting go of the old. Exactly what I'm doing." Annie was speaking more to herself than Paula. Realizing it, she turned to her friend and smiled. "It's not always so easy." And then with a determined grimace she added, "But I'm going to do it. So let's load up your car with this stuff before you change your mind."

Later, exhausted and sweaty, Annie waved good-bye to Paula, whose car was so loaded down by the weight of all those boxes that its bottom barely cleared the road.

Out with the old, in with the new, Annie said to herself as she walked back to her apartment. Now if she could only find some way to cart off her disturbing thoughts about Nick. It was one thing to tell him the past was over, but as Paula said, she was a packrat. She saved everything.

And it wasn't only things she had a hard time letting go of. Feelings clung to her like glue. Feelings for Nick stuck harder than most.

It had been much easier before he'd shown up. Oh, she had known one of these days they'd meet up again, but not under these circumstances. She never dreamed Nick would appear at her doorstep, injured and wanting her help. A stab of conscience struck her. Then a rush of common sense. She'd made the only decision possible.

Nick decided, as Bill Kenny bandaged his ankle, that at least he could be grateful to Annie for one thing. Since he'd hobbled out of her office two days ago, he had been so preoccupied with thoughts about her that his pain had taken a back seat. Now as he sat in his dressing room trying to psych himself up for the finals match, he found that the old fire was surprisingly missing. Usually before a big event he had to contain the blaze of heat and energy flowing through his body, channeling it carefully to carry him through the long, intense match. Today, the few sparks he felt were forced.

Bill Kenny was holding out a couple of painkillers for him. Nick shook his head. There had been a few bad times when he'd taken them, but he was judicious about their use. Nick had seen too many athletes come to depend on pills to keep them going. He had no intention of joining their leagues. If he couldn't make it on his own steam, then Annie was right—it would be time to hang up the old racket. He was still convinced she was wrong.

The argument had been going on in his mind since he'd left her office. He kept telling himself she had overstated the problem, made it out to be more of a crisis than it was. After all, look at him now. His ankle wasn't causing a twinge. Of course he refused to consider how it was going to feel at the end of today's match. The argument might then lead dangerously in Annie's favor.

He cursed himself for having gone there. When she'd disappeared in the crowds last week as he'd started up the stands toward her, he should have gotten the message. And he should have let it be. Nick knew Annie too well to imagine she would easily bury the hatchet. He had been riding on false hope when he went to her office. And he had let himself in for it. Maybe I was asking for exactly what I got, he thought. Ten months of feeling like a total heel wasn't very pleasant. Maybe, he'd thought, if I let her have another go at telling me off, I'll feel absolved. But it hadn't worked; he felt even worse.

When Annie had first blown up about that article announcing his pending engagement to Lynn, Nick tried to make her see that it was simply another PR tack. He admitted that before Annie came into the picture the idea of marrying Lynn was not totally out in left field. But since he and Annie had been involved his only contacts with Lynn had been for the gossip columns. It kept the fans charged up and that was part of Nick's job.

It hadn't seemed so awful to Nick, but Annie had seen it very differently. She didn't believe the papers would print that kind of news unless there was some smoke. When he'd tried to defend himself, she'd told him she had no doubt that he would probably marry Lynn if his agent told him it would sell some more tickets to his game.

Nick was as angry as Annie at first. He felt he was being wrongly attacked. But he also knew it had been a big mistake not to tell Annie anything about his real relationship with Lynn. Feelings that he had either shoved aside or been too busy to think about had come back in a flood of sensations when he'd caught sight of Annie the other day. And they hadn't left him since.

At first he had thought about using his ankle as an excuse to see her again. Then, in his dressing room after the match with Norrison, he realized it would not really be an excuse. He had been avoiding doctors like the plague. He was scared. Annie, showing up as she did, seemed like an act of Providence.

Things didn't work out as he had expected. She had told him exactly what he hadn't wanted to hear, and she had reawakened all of those X-rated fantasies he thought he had finally gotten under control. She had also given him a taste of his own medicine, to boot. One very large tablespoon of bitter rejection. It had not gone down well.

"Do you want to walk around on it a bit?" Bill Kenny asked him.

"Huh? Oh, yeah, sure, Bill." He slid off the table, crossed the room and came back. "Feels good. Real good."

"The swelling has gone down. Shouldn't cause you too much of a problem today. Might want to take a couple of pills just to be on the safe side." Bill knew Nick hated taking pain-killers but he was also around when Winters limped off the courts after a match. No reason to suffer more than you had to.

"No, Bill. I'm fine. This match is going to be a breeze. I won't need to be doing any fancy leaps with Leyland. He just had a lucky break the other day. He's probably as surprised as I am that he's in the finals today."

As he talked he did some stretching work. His ankle was a little tender, but plenty better than some other days. He began concentrating on the match. The adrenaline was beginning to flow, and by the time Stu MacKenzie got there, the old confidence and control was settling nicely into place.

Stu MacKenzie, known to everyone as Mac, had been Nick's coach since the time Nick first entered the pro circuit. From the minute Mac had begun working with the young firebrand, he knew he was witnessing the flowering of an extraordinary talent. Instead of trying to teach Nick to contain his explosive personality, he taught him how to make it work for him. For all Nick's high-strung, intensely charged nature on

45

court, Mac was one of the privileged few who had experienced Nick's gentler side. Nick respected Mac, worked his butt off for him, and Mac never took advantage of their genuine friendship for each other. Not that their relationship had been smooth sailing over the years. They locked horns all the time, Mac having the ability to be as explosive and critical as Nick. Still, they both always managed to come out of their battles intact—Nick invariably playing better and with even greater skill.

Lately Mac had been worried about his boy. He had encouraged Nick more times than he could count to get some medical attention. He had given up telling him to slow down. Nick always overbooked his schedule, never giving himself a chance to rest his bruised, aching body. This year, as Nick's playing had become erratic, he seemed more determined than ever to enter every damn tournament that came along.

Mac was pleased to see Nick looking so good today. He watched for a while as Nick went through his routine warmup.

"Feeling good—huh?" Mac grunted, circling around Nick. He reached out and grabbed his player's wrist. The coach was nearly a head shorter than Nick, a wiry, fleet-footed man who was much stronger than he appeared. His grip was like steel.

"Loose, buddy. Keep that old wrist nice and flexible. You tightened up too much in the semis."

"I won the semis." Nick grinned.

"You could have won better," the coach said, grinning back. "Today you are going to have to work for that silver cup, hotshot. You sure you got it in you? Those old bones ain't creaking too much?" Mac kept it light and bantering but all the while he was watching for any signs of problems. He looked down with an intentional grimace at Nick's bandaged ankle. Nick followed his gaze.

"Never fear, Mac. My old bones have never been better." Nick slapped his coach lightly on the shoulder. "Do you want to talk bones all day or are we going to get down to business? Maybe you think I don't need any last-minute instructions."

Mac emitted another of his famous grunts and then the two of them settled down to the work at hand. By the time Mac left, Nick could practically feel the winner's cup in the palm of his hand. He visualized Leyland's loping style, his tendency to rush his swings—especially when he was nervous. And playing Wild Man Winters was going to make him nervous. That suited Nick just fine. The electric energy was building and Nick carefully nursed it for the ensuing confrontation. He was ready to chalk up another victory—and prove to Annie Kneeland that this boy wasn't ready to be put out to meadow. Not by a long shot.

Her desk was almost cleared. The office was beginning to look impersonal and uninhabited.

In two more days it would be. The new doctor wasn't arriving for a couple of weeks. After sifting through a last pile of notes Annie leaned back in her chair and yawned. She had slept fitfully the night before. Hearing Nick's name on the eleven o'clock news hadn't helped matters any. He had won the match against Leyland. Annie wasn't surprised. When she found herself starting to wonder how much pain he was in, she pulled up the covers over her head and tried to get to sleep. She didn't have much success.

When Paula buzzed to say that a Mr. Grimes was here to see her, Annie couldn't imagine who he was. She had terminated her work with all of her patients. Paula was equally in the dark, but indicated that Mr. Grimes was very insistent. Annie asked her to send him to her office.

"Thank you for seeing me, Dr. Kneeland." Mr. Grimes extended his hand formally and then immediately reached into his inner breast pocket for a card which he presented crisply to Annie.

Annie studied the card and then looked back up at the presenter, an exceedingly tall, imposing-looking gentleman, in his fifties, Annie estimated, who looked as though he had just stepped out of a Brooks Brothers' clothing ad. Annie barely reached his shoulders. She asked him to sit down.

"I'm afraid I'm not familiar with Centurion Enterprises, Mr. Grimes." She glanced at the card again and then placed it on her desk.

"Centurian Enterprises is a very renowned public relations firm, Doctor. We handle the top athletes in the country. Nick Winters is ours." He spoke in a clipped, affected style that Annie found irritating. She particularly did not like the way he claimed ownership of Nick. She was about to tell him that she hadn't noticed Centurion's brand burned into Nick's hide when she'd examined him, but Mr. Grimes was already speaking again.

"We understand Winters came to see you on Monday. May I ask precisely what was the nature of his business here?" He gave her a brief smile that showed his pearly whites for a fleeting moment. She guessed this was supposed to engender confidence, thus encouraging her to speak openly. It didn't.

"Mr. Grimes, are you sure you handed me the right card? I may be reading too many books, but you sound more FBI than PR. Has Mr. Winters committed some crime?"

"Forgive me, Doctor." He forced a dry laugh. "I assure you I am who I say I am. And I do understand the privileged communication between doctor and patient. Of course, if Mr. Winters was here as a patient . . ." He let the sentence hang.

He was wily, this Mr. Grimes. Annie leaned back in her swivel seat. "Really, Mr. Grimes, anything I might say obviously would be breaching a confidence. And since, as you say, you understand, I can't see any purpose to our discussion. I would think that it's Mr. Winters you ought to be having this talk with."

"I seem to have gotten off on the wrong foot, Dr. Kneeland. Probably read too many books myself." He tried for another laugh. It was tight and self-conscious. "I'm here out of concern, very deep-felt concern, for Mr. Winters. Actually I am hoping he was here for treatment. You see, we have been aware for quite a while that Nick has not been feeling up to par, not playing with the old gusto. Something is wrong. Bill Kenny, his trainer, has informed us that he's been particularly bothered by some old injuries to his ankles. We don't know if other problems may be causing him pain as well. As I say, we are concerned." He made a firm effort this time to make his smile more ingratiating. He wasn't successful as far as Annie was concerned.

"You also must have a great deal invested in Mr. Winters. Owning a man like him must involve quite a few pennies. But then, I'm sure he's a very valuable asset," Annie said coolly. They had definitely sent the wrong man out for the job.

Grimes picked this up, too. He decided to stop working so hard at winning confidence and got down to brass tacks.

"I am going to assume, Doctor, that Winters came here for medical advice. I'm well aware that the two of you were very close not terribly long ago. And that you had some kind of a rift. So I doubt Nick merely dropped into your office to say hi."

Annie was livid. "You had us followed? How dare you . . ." Then, catching her breath, she said, "This is sounding more like the FBI by the minute."

"We got where we are by always protecting our investments. And we do have a lot invested in Mr. Winters. He has current contracts endorsing everything from tennis rackets to yogurt. And we are working on even more lucrative deals for the upcoming year. I'm sure you know that those deals depend very much on Nick Winters's health. Our concern is to keep him well and winning. And we are prepared to do whatever is necessary to see that that is accomplished. I am here to find out if you have any suggestions as to how we might do that best."

Annie decided she would just throw out a few feelers to test Mr. Grimes's level of concern. Not that she didn't already know its depth. Probably went just as far down as his coffers—which would stay nice and full as long as Nick was out there filling them for him.

"What if I told you, Mr. Grimes, that Nick Winters's well-being would be best accomplished if he quit playing so much tennis. Or"—she paused, eyeing the slightly red-faced man with disdain—"that he should quit altogether."

"I doubt that Nick Winters would accept that advice, Doctor," he said with a smile.

This smile grated her even more than his previous ones. "All I can do is offer medical advice," Annie said icily. "I could offer you some apt advice as well. . . ." She stopped, annoyed

51

that she was letting this irritating man get to her.

"Doctor, I came here today with all good intentions. I had hoped that you might be able to help Nick, and my company wanted to back that all the way. In my pocket I have a very impressive contract offering you a job as Nick Winters's personal physician. Since he chose you in the first place, we assume he has the utmost confidence in you. And since you are an old and dear friend, his health would be of even greater concern to you."

Annie started to speak, but Grimes put up his hand quickly. "Before you tell me where to put my contract, Doctor, let's consider all of the aspects of the situation. First of all we are well aware that you are leaving this medical facility and will not be starting at your new job for several months. If my sources are correct, you are planning a vacation. What could be a better choice than traveling to all the scenic spots in Europe? I'm sure Mr. Winters's ailments will not occupy all of your time." He could tell from her scowl that this argument was not going to be effective. He switched tactics. "This contract, besides offering—uhm, let us say, generous compensation for your services, also provides a very substantial financial contribution to the orthopedic unit at St. Mead's Hospital in New York. I believe the facilities there do not begin to compare with this place, and they could certainly benefit from a hefty donation."

"You've really thought of everything, Mr.

Grimes. Except for one little fact. I don't take bribes. I'm afraid you've wasted both our mornings." If she weren't so angry, that donation might have had some persuasive pull. St. Mead's could certainly use the money. But her guilt at refusing the offer was meager in comparison to her outrage.

"You surprise me, Doctor. Oh, not the bribe business. But I thought you might be concerned about a man whom you once apparently cared a great deal about. He'll never agree to another doctor, you know. Unfortunately that leaves little else but pain-killers to get Nick through the season. It is scary, Doctor, to see athletes forced to take that path. But then, working here, I imagine you are already familiar with the devastating consequences of that kind of recourse."

When he gazed across the desk at her he kept his face completely deadpan. But he knew he had her. Herb Grimes had just scored another success in a long and prosperous career.

CHAPTER THREE

The final meeting with Doug Fisher had gone better than she'd expected. After her morning encounter with Herb Grimes, Annie was in a lousy mood.

Buffaloed, that's what had happened. Grimes had thrown out the lasso and she'd stepped right in. Good-bye vacation. Good-bye common sense. She'd signed her John Hancock on the dotted line, agreeing to a four-month stint with the devil. Don't tell me Santa Claus and fate exist after all, she'd thought wryly after Grimes had walked out.

Nick had managed to get his way in the end. Although she was certain Nick had not sent Grimes over—Nick never sent others to do his bidding—he had nonetheless achieved his end. Annie would be following him around the globe administering to his aches. But that was absolutely all she intended to administer to. At the end of four months she was bound and determined to wave good-bye without so much as a fleeting regret and go about her own plans. And she refused to have to nurse any personal wounds in the process.

Either Doug Fisher had sensed Annie was still doing a slow boil or else he figured it was senseless to carry the grudge to the bitter end—whatever his reason, he was pleasant and supportive in that officious style Annie knew so well. She politely accepted Fisher's well-wishes, tolerated his parting words of wisdom, and was grateful for the fact that he was going to be out of town during her last two days of work.

When she returned to her office she dialed the Delray Beach tennis club and got Nick's hotel number. He wasn't in. She knew her relief was only temporary. Leaving a message for him to meet her for dinner at the Harborside, a popular Delray Beach restaurant, she hung up and tried to figure out just how she was going to tell Nick she had decided to take on the job as his physician after all.

Her keys jangled discordantly on the metal ring around her index finger as she stepped outside the clinic a couple of hours later. Patches of concrete were still wet from a brief afternoon shower, but the scorching sun was drying it off rapidly. The air was thick and steamy. Annie stepped around a small puddle in the parking lot.

Nick's Porsche was blocking her car.

"Want a lift?"

"We were supposed to meet at the restaurant." She had been planning to spend the time driving alone to get her thoughts in order. She wasn't prepared to see him yet.

When Nick had picked up the message from Annie at his hotel he'd driven right over to her office. He'd been waiting outside for nearly half an hour. But he didn't want to give Annie a chance to back out. "I wasn't sure of the way," he said with a grin.

Annie grinned back. Nick was famous for getting lost. Annie used to tease him about having the worst sense of direction she'd ever witnessed. It had been a running joke.

Nick opened the passenger door of his sports car. For a moment as she slid in beside him, memories of another time washed over them, their eyes meeting in shared remembrance. Nick's gaze lingered, a warming smile suffusing his features. He still couldn't believe she had actually decided to go out to dinner with him.

Annie continued to struggle with telling Nick about her change of heart concerning his medical care. If she simply told him she'd reconsidered, he could easily jump to the wrong conclusions. On the other hand Annie was quite certain that Nick would be livid if she recounted her disquieting conversation with the unpleasant Mr. Grimes. It was one of those no-win situations. And the truth was, both options led to the same place—her heart. She cared about Nick. She told herself she had gotten over her attraction, her anger, and her hurt. She told herself that Nick's devastating sexual appeal had no part in her decision. She told herself that she was merely responding to the old Hippocratic oath. She even tried to convince herself the donation to the hospital had been the deciding factor. She ended up telling herself she was a miserable liar.

"Nick, I've been thinking about—about your ankle."

"Only my ankle?" he quipped, glancing over at her with a grin.

"Can we have a serious conversation?" Annie sighed, wondering for the hundredth time how she'd ever got herself into this whole thing. "I still think you're crazy not to put yourself in the hospital, but, then, I've always known you lack common sense. You're stubborn, arrogant, and no doubt convinced you're indestructible."

"You do know how to give a compliment, Doc. Are you saving the best for last?"

"And that's another thing, Nick. If I'm going to look after your battered body, you are going to have to quit the banter. Because, believe me, buddy, I'm a hard-nosed doctor and I do not play games with patients. You either follow my orders or you can take your aching ankle and . . ."

"Are you trying to tell me in that inimitable fashion of yours, Dr. Kneeland, that you are going to traipse around the world with me after all?" Nick had parked the car against the curb.

"I never was very good at vacationing. Might as well keep in practice until I start at St. Mead's. After I've coped with you for a few months, the kids at the hospital will be a breeze."

"Now who's playing games? Come on, Anna Falanna." His hand nonchalantly toyed with a strand of her hair. Annie abruptly turned her head.

"Okay, what happens to you matters to me. I don't want to see you crippled for life. That's not so difficult to understand. I'd feel the same way about anyone I'd known since I was in diapers. But let's be clear about something, Nick. I intend to treat this stint in purely professional terms. I'm only agreeing to be your doctor. And I meant what I said—if you don't follow my treatment plan, I will head right back home."

Nick surprised her. She expected one of his snappy comebacks. Instead his voice was startlingly earnest as he turned his face to her.

"I meant what I said, too, Annie. I need you. I don't trust many people and I've spent too many years learning that honest caring doesn't pop up that often. Everyone has an angle and I've become an important commodity. Stardom has its drawbacks."

"If you feel that way why keep going through all this? There are other things in life besides tennis." Nick didn't say anything, but Annie hadn't expected an answer. She already knew the answer.

Since they were children, Nick had always been out to prove himself. He was driven to compete, to succeed. Those needs had consumed him for so long, they had become an integral part of everything he did. And tennis had provided the outlet for both his competitive nature and his superb athletic skill. It had also been his life, his whole life, for a such a long time that Annie realized he probably never allowed any other possibilities to enter his mind. The whole notion of youngsters being guided and molded into careers before they could fully understand what that meant, disturbed Annie. She had almost followed the same path as Nick. Had she been as talented, had the promotors and PR people singled her out as golden, maybe she would have been swallowed up by it all, too. The money, the glamor, the cheering crowds—fame was difficult to reject. Even later, when you learned the price fame cost, it was no easier to relinquish.

As they walked toward the small seaside restaurant Nick told Annie he would have his coach call her and arrange the details of her contract. Annie almost slipped. She was about to tell Nick that wouldn't be necessary. She made a mental note to give Mac a call as soon as she got back home, telling him the truth, and explaining that she did not think it would be good for Nick to know about Grimes. She knew Mac well enough from the old days to know she could trust him to do what was best for Nick.

When they stepped inside the restaurant, Nick asked for a table by the window. When they were seated he looked out at the colorful array of boats gently bobbing in the harbor. His mind matched the motion, thoughts floating disjointedly about in his head. Relief mingled with tension, those feelings overshadowed by an ever-growing desire. Annie sparked more fire-works than the Fourth of July. While she busied herself fixing his busted ankle, she might end up causing him other more fundamental distress.

"Pretty sight," Annie said. "A perfect Florida seascape."

"Are you going to miss it?" Nick asked, shifting his gaze to Annie, studying her with curiosity. Why was she leaving here? he wondered. She seemed so right somehow for the setting, the beauty of the surroundings a fitting backdrop for her loveliness.

"A part of me will miss it. It's an easy way of life. Not that the work at the center hasn't been hard or challenging, but the elegance and wealth that are part and parcel of the place lend it an air of unreality. I guess it sounds strange, but the truth is I don't feel connected here. I don't feel that I'm growing or that I'm a part of the mainstream of life. I want that feeling. It's very important to me. Life has been too easy for people like us, Nick. We grew up in a kind of make-believe world where money and social status seemed to take care of everything. So safe and secure. There's an inherent danger in that kind of world. It's easy to forget that there are an awful lot of people out there busy struggling with the harsh realities of a far less advantaged life."

She hadn't meant to go on like that. Those feelings had existed inside of her for a long time, but she rarely spoke about them. "Forgive the sermon," Annie said with a laugh. She was sure Nick would tease her for her earnestness.

Instead he said, "You're quite a woman, Annie. But then you always had a special sensitivity even as a young girl. I wish I hadn't taken it so much for granted."

Annie flushed. "Oversensitive more often than not." She paused for a moment and then looked directly at Nick. "If I'm going to work with you, I think we'd better clear the air. What happened last year between us was doomed from the start. It wasn't only Lynn. We were fooling ourselves believing we could bridge the distance between us." She stared bleakly at him, the memory of their involvement only serving to refresh the pain.

"Annie, I wanted to tell you the truth. Sometimes in this business, you don't seem to matter except as a commodity. The press has been pursuing me for years, writing all kinds of stories, most of them planted by my publicity agent. I stopped reading them years ago. Lynn and I were thrown together because we made such great copy. Maybe for a while there we both believed it. But not after you."

"My point is you've allowed yourself to be a commodity. You let the whole thing with Lynn happen. Probably with her willing cooperation. She's a big commodity, too. I hate the whole thing. Don't you understand? You're so totally immersed in it all you can't even see it clearly."

"I see one thing clearly. I've hurt you badly.

I promise never to hurt you intentionally again, Annie."

"I promise not to give you the opportunity," Annie said. "Don't misunderstand me, Nick. Letting bygones be bygones simply means I'm going to stop throwing daggers. I'm not looking to start anything."

"I hear you, Annie. I don't completely believe you, but I hear you."

"Nick . . ."

"I think we should table both the past and the future for a while and stick with the present for now. What are you going to eat?" He grinned, lifting his menu from the table.

They ordered their dinners and while they waited Annie asked Nick about his upcoming schedule.

"The doubles finals are tomorrow and then it's rest time until the fourteenth, when we play in Gstaad for the Swiss Open."

"How is Jeff Reese doing? He is still your doubles partner?" Annie had met Jeff after she started getting seriously involved in tennis. He was another young up-and-comer, but Jeff's style, personality, and background were on the opposite end of the spectrum from Nick's. Jeff learned his tennis in school playgrounds, but what he lacked in refinement and skill he made up for in sheer determination. Jeff never made any bones about the fact that he was playing for the money. He'd been poor all his life and he had no intention of staying that way. He and Nick used to practice together and early on they teamed up for doubles matches. Jeff had never become a superstar, but he and Nick together had been ranked first in doubles for the last six years.

"He's still the same. Except that he got himself hitched last year. A regular old married man."

"Jeff Reese married? That's a hard one to imagine. He never seemed the type for settling down."

"Who said anything about settling down?" Nick teased.

"How innocent of me," Annie said tartly.

"I'm joking. Jeff's true blue. Or at least a reasonable facsimile. Unfortunately Barbara, his wife, has a problem with color-blindness. She's not the trusting sort."

"I can understand that," Annie countered. "Jeff is constantly off in exotic places surrounded by the adulation of fans, treated royally. Celibacy must come hard after so many years of sexual freedom. Maybe Jeff's wife is afraid temptations aren't easily ignored."

"Things can get tough." Nick grinned. "But not every piece of candy turns out to be as good as it looks. And I think Jeff has sampled enough candy in his day to know that. Barbara would be wiser to let up on the jealousy bit or she may string her man too tight."

"You don't like her very much," Annie observed, intentionally avoiding his gibe referring to women as candy. She was not about to give him the satisfaction of getting her goat.

"Actually, when she's not playing the role of suspicious wife, she's a great lady. She's down to earth, funny, honest. A lot like Jeff, actually. But where he's cool and controlled she's got her emotions spread out all over the place. You are right about one thing. I think Barbara would be far happier if Jeff wasn't always on the move. That's always tough on a marriage. Tennis stars are not exempt from the high divorce rate by a long shot."

"Another price of fame and fortune," Annie said cynically. Nick was right. Stardom did not enhance intimate relationships. She was going to make sure she kept that in mind.

"The costs do have a way of escalating," Nick agreed. He, too, planned to keep in mind that his life was complicated enough right now. He had a feeling Annie was going to make it tougher.

They might have both relaxed more if they knew how strongly they each wanted to protect themselves—and if they could have believed it.

Officially she did not begin her new job as Nick's physician until they got to Switzerland, but Annie had insisted on checking his ankle carefully in the dressing room before his doubles match in Delray Beach. She sensed that Nick's trainer was a little annoyed about being replaced, but when she saw the array of painkillers on his table she did not concern herself with his disgruntlement. When Kenny went off to administer to someone else Annie bandaged Nick's ankle.

"How often do you take those pain-killers Kenny dishes out?" Annie snapped as she secured the wrapping more tightly than she meant.

"Hey, take it easy. Are you planning to shut off circulation as a new cure?" Nick put his hand on Annie's shoulder. "I don't pop pills."

"It's the worse thing you could do. Not only because they're all too easy to get dependent on, but if you're doped up and feeling no pain, you could end up injuring yourself more without even knowing."

Nick's hand still rested on her shoulder. "Annie, you're wound tighter than I am right now. Which reminds me, let up on the bandage a little, huh?"

"Sorry," she murmured, reaching for his leg. Nick's hand stopped her.

"But first, relax. I'm going to be fine. My ankle looks good, I've taken it nice and easy for two days, and Jeff and I are going to go out there and play a pleasant, leisurely game of gentleman's tennis." His gray eyes sparkled with amusement.

"Whoever said tennis was a gentleman's sport needs his head examined," Annie retorted. "There's far too much money and glory at stake for players to be gentlemen. Tennis is as cutthroat and tough as they come, Mr. Winters. And you"—she thumbed her finger into his solar plexus—"lead the pack."

"Well, do I at least get a good-luck kiss before I go out there and bare my teeth, Doc?" Nick teased. Only he wasn't really teasing. He was having a hard time fighting his impulse to take her in his arms. The memory of Annie's response to his last kiss continued to haunt him. He slipped his arm around her waist.

Annie didn't struggle but Nick could feel her muscles tighten in defense. Before she said a word, he dropped his arm.

"I got carried away." He looked at her wistfully.

She nodded silently.

Things seemed to have a way of not going according to plan where she and Nick were concerned. Without thinking, Annie leaned forward and pressed her lips to his. As she knew he would, his arms encircled her and he brought her closer, not releasing her until she had been kissed fully. His eyes held hers as he let her go, a dark smoldering gleam in the grayness. Then he smiled, his eyes lightening, the smile softening the hungry set of his lips.

"I got carried away," she echoed with a whisper of a laugh. "Good luck out there." Then she started toward the door, stopping before she reached it. "Watch that ankle, Winters. Or there'll be hell to pay." She threw him her most reproachful look.

Nick winked. "I'll behave, Doc." As she opened the door he couldn't resist adding, "On the court."

* * *

66

"Forty–thirty."

Annie watched Nick and Jeff dazzle the crowds with their spectacular, perfectly synchronized performance. They had played together for so many years as to have almost choreographed their exquisitely timed movements.

When she arrived in the stands Annie's head was spinning and she missed the first few plays. She was dumbfounded by what she had done. Nick had gallantly backed off and instead of breathing a sigh of relief, she had been stung by disappointment. Annie had wanted that kiss. Impulsively she had taken it. So much for good intentions and fair warnings.

She finally managed to focus her attention on the game, consoling herself that it wasn't too late to get a firmer hold of her impulses. Still, even with renewed resolve in place, she had difficulty getting into the pure excitement of the match, her concern switching from self-chastisement to worry. Every time Nick took a leap or switched directions abruptly, Annie's pulse raced, her eyes watchfully checking out his face for signs of pain or distress. Any move, however innocuous it might seem at the moment, could cause a serious problem. Nick had been lucky so far. The pain notwithstanding, his ankle could, by all rights should, be in far worse shape than it was. Annie was determined to do everything in her power to make sure his luck held out.

For all her speeches and advice about his quitting the profession, she knew how much the next few months meant to Nick. As long as he followed her treatment plan and cut back on his schedule—and as long as his luck held out—he would make it to Wimbledon on two feet. Hopefully he would walk off that way as well.

They were just beginning the fourth set. Nick was serving, Jeff at net. Belton and Morrisey had taken the second set. They were a fine pair of players and a real challenge. Yet Nick and Jeff held two sets to one, and it was clear from the way they were playing that they were confident of a win.

Belton went for broke on Nick's serve, returning the ball deep in the backhand corner. Nick sprang for it, smashing the ball with such force cross-court that Morrisey never stood a chance of returning it. An exquisite shot; the crowd applauded enthusiastically. Jeff glanced back at Nick with a smile of appreciation.

Only Nick didn't smile back. His face was set in a tight grimace. When Jeff's expression switched to concern, Nick merely nodded that he was okay.

He wasn't. That last sprint had caused a sharp, stabbing pain that shot from his ankle right up to his thigh. He was in agony, trying desperately to loosen the muscles and somehow ease the pressure. He did a few runs in place, the pain abating a little.

Annie made a beeline down the stands to Nick's coach. Mac was sitting in the first row.

Slightly out of breath, Annie squeezed across the aisle.

"Nick's done something to his leg out there. Call him in, Mac. Find out what's going on." The words spewed out of her mouth.

"Slow down, Annie. I saw that play, but he seems to have worked it out. Probably just a pull. I'll check with him when they switch courts." Mac moved over one seat, making room for Annie to sit. He knew Annie from her tennis days and when Nick told him she was coming along as his physician, Mac was pleased. Still, he couldn't have his boy coddled, pulled out of a big match for every muscle ache. As far as he could see Nick was okay.

Annie knew better. Nick was hurting. There was no doubt of it. He was also adept at hiding pain. He would have to fall over unconscious before he'd concede a match due to an injury. It was madness. Annie felt angry and hopeless.

When the teams changed sides, Mac had a quiet word with Nick. Annie saw Nick's intense expression, heard him growl that he was fine, and watched Mac shrug his shoulders.

It was downhill from there. Nick started chopping the ball too much, missing easy shots when they required swift footwork, in general not connecting early enough. By this time Mac was equally aware that Nick had to be hurting to be doing such a rotten job.

Belton and Morrisey changed tactics as they saw Nick losing ground. Jeff worked hard to compensate for Nick's errors but it was a downhill struggle.

It was an exciting upset. The crowd, always

69

enthusiastic about the underdogs coming out on top, applauded vigorously. Annie hurried down to the locker room. A group of reporters were bombarding Nick and Jeff with questions. When you're the number-one players, you're expected to win. If you don't everyone wants to know what went wrong. Nick was the real one on trial. He was the superstar, the king. The press had been on his back all year. His losses were big news, bigger than his wins. Those were expected. Nick had consistently remained close-mouthed about the cause of his problems this season. No matter how often reporters asked what was wrong, Nick's answer was always the same. The other guy played better than he did —short and simple. The press weren't about to settle for such dull copy. Was he suffering some emotional problems, physical difficulties; was it a woman or gambling behind his surprising losses; was he on the take? They never let up. Nick never lost his cool.

Until today. Maybe the badgering had gone too far or maybe the pain was too intense. Whatever the reason, Nick had reached the breaking point. A half-dozen reporters were crowding in on him, throwing questions around like a volley ball. Suddenly Nick grabbed the guy closest to him, lifted him right off the floor, and threw him against the wall. Then he broke through the group and stormed down the hall. The reporters were an excited swarm of buzzing bees. This was great copy. Up to now Nick Winters had saved his abusive style for the courts. Now he was providing his special brand of excitement off court and the press loved it—even the poor guy who had gotten nailed to the wall.

Nick slammed the door to the locker room. Annie, who had been only two feet from the door, waited a minute and then followed him in. Jeff, already inside, was trying to talk to Nick, only Nick wasn't answering. Mac came in to the room on Annie's heels. He, too, approached Nick. Both men quickly sensed that this was not the time to push. They looked over at Annie, who had stayed near the door. She signaled them with her eyes and they left on cue.

Nick sat on a hard wooden chair, his head in his hands. He didn't want sympathy and he didn't want questions. Annie walked over and in a cool, professional voice ordered him over to the table. He gave her one of his sulkily hooded gazes and then silently did what he was told.

Neither of them spoke. Annie could spot the swelling even before she removed his shoe and sock. She immediately applied an ice pack to the tender area. It was imperative to bring the swelling down as swiftly as possible. Annie could only guess at how much pain Nick was in. Plenty. But Nick was stoic, letting Annie put mild pressure on the injury without so much as a moan.

She wrapped the ice pack around the ankle, gently propping his leg on a pillow. The pain was beginning to fade a bit. Nick's eyes met Annie's.

"Where's the tirade, Doc? Aren't you going to tell me what a dumb fool I am?"

"I could come up with far better adjectives," she answered, a thin smile curving her lips, "but something tells me you've already told yourself everything I could throw at you."

"You're right." He managed a grin despite the throbbing pain.

Annie walked over to her medical bag and came back with a vial of pills. She shook out two tablets and handed them to Nick.

"I thought you didn't approve of pills."

"These are anti-inflammatories. We've got to bring the swelling down before I can really figure out just how bad this is." She was back to using her professional voice again.

She handed Nick a glass of water and watched him swallow the tablets. After she'd done everything possible for the moment, she hopped up on the table next to Nick.

"I do admit, Anna Falanna, that sometimes I think it just isn't worth it." Nick didn't look at her as he spoke but he could feel her eyes on him. Eyes as blue as the ocean and he didn't have to see them to know they refected compassion. Her slender hand rested on her knee. He placed his own hand over hers. She took hold of his fingers, squeezing gently.

He could feel tears misting his eyes. He wasn't sure whether it was the physical pain that refused to let up or the emotional impact of Annie's tender care that had triggered the response. He did know that having her here with him now felt more important than anything else in the world. He slipped his arm around her.

Annie rested her head on his shoulder. Her defenses seemed to slip away. No matter how hard she denied it, or how hard she fought it, the bond was there. Time couldn't alter it any more than pain or anger—or fear. And deep down Annie was afraid—afraid she was heading right back into another match, and she was certain she couldn't win this one, either. Nick was far too tough an opponent. Yet she found herself entering the court despite the poor odds.

Nick turned and gazed at her for a long moment. Still holding her hand he slipped his fingers through hers and smiled as she brought his hand to her lips.

"Let's go, Annie."

A simple request, his words held a complexity of emotions and desires. He lifted her down off the table, Annie's lips curving into a smile that traveled to her eyes. Eyes as blue as the sea. She nodded, the smile lighting up the darkness that had been shadowing Nick for a long time.

CHAPTER FOUR

Nick's arm was slung lightly over Annie's shoulder as she drove the BMW to her apartment. At least it was hers until tomorrow when the movers came to cart her furniture into storage for the next four months and she returned her key to the landlord. Nick was silent during the trip. Annie knew he was in a lot of pain, but his face was set in a determined grimace to keep it to himself.

Annie was right. Nick was hurting. He was also scared. He couldn't figure it out. Last year when he and Annie were together he didn't recall feeling so—so threatened. Then again, last year he was in top form, physically and emotionally. And now . . .

Now he was depending on Annie in ways he never had. That was the crux of the matter. He was feeling dependent on her. It wasn't only his need to have her care for him medically, somehow getting him through this grueling season. It went deeper than that. His need for her had an almost spiritual quality. Her presence seemed to soothe his soul as well as his body. It felt good and at the same time it was terrifying. Nick Winters had always wanted, but never before really needed, anybody. Only tennis. That was the one thing he had accepted needing. Winning—being a champion—had nurtured him all these years. And this year . . .

This year was his last hurrah. It was his final chance. And he was determined to go out a winner. He had tried not to accept the reality of nearing the end to a career that had given him so much of what he craved. He had tried to bury his fears and anxieties about the future. Whenever he saw old pros hawking products on TV he felt a depressing sadness. It was one thing to be in front of a camera when you were in your glory. It was quite another to know that everyone watching was thinking, "Oh, so that's what became of that guy."

Annie thought Nick was asleep. She tapped him lightly on the shoulder.

"We're here."

Nick opened his eyes. Annie was startled by the look of desolation in his gaze.

"Nick, it isn't too bad," she said gently.

For a moment Nick thought she'd been reading his mind and he felt even more threatened. Then he realized she was simply referring to his ankle. With all the other feelings bombarding him, he'd almost forgotten the still-throbbing pain.

"I have total confidence in your healing powers, Doc." He managed a smile. It faded as he stepped out of the car and tried to put some pressure on the injured foot.

"Hold on," Annie ordered, swinging his arm around her shoulder and forcing him to let her bear some of his weight.

"You're nice to lean on," he murmured seductively, pushing aside his nagging feeling of dependency.

Annie was not a mind reader, but she didn't have to be to know that Nick Winters did not like having to lean on anyone—unless he was in control. Annie decided to ignore the innuendoes Nick was throwing. He was in no condition to act on them anyway. Then again, Nick could tolerate a great deal of pain when he was going after something he wanted. She would have to watch her step after all.

"Nice place you've got here. Did you design it yourself or did you hire the local wrecking crew to decorate?"

Annie laughed. "Believe it or not, this apartment used to be a real showplace. Well, maybe that's going a bit too far. But it was homey."

Annie had moved into this apartment shortly after she and Nick broke up. She had told herself at the time that she needed a larger place—all the junk she always accumulated took up half the space—but the truth was her old apartment held too many memories. She still remembered all those nights when Nick flew in late from some tournament or other, and they'd have a romantic midnight dinner and then feast on each other till morning.

This place belonged only to her. Right now that thought made her feel more secure.

"I liked your other place better." Nick was not going to make this thing easy. "I used to get a kick out of all the things you'd manage to collect in each of my absences. Remember how you used to dig everything out and throw them on the bed? Funny . . ." His words drifted off, but not his thoughts. Those were good times—the best.

"Nick, don't."

He walked toward her. "We could have made it, Annie."

"No." She shook her head sadly. The light touch of his hands on her shoulders made her shiver involuntarily. She moved away.

Her back to him, she rummaged through her medical bag and drew out a vial of pills. Setting them on the table, she said, in as professional a voice as she could manage, "You're only here tonight so I can take care of that ankle. I told you our relationship was going to be strictly professional and I meant it, Nick. And if you give me any guff, I'll send you hobbling back to your hotel and you can take that plane to Gstaad tomorrow night alone."

"Sorry, Doc. I'll cooperate," he said contritely, but Annie did not miss the sparkle of mischief in his eye.

"Sit down on the couch and let me see if the swelling has gone down any."

Nick had to move a few boxes off the couch before he could comply with her orders. Sitting quietly he let Annie roll up his cuff and remove the Ace bandage. He watched her as she examined him. Her cool, slender fingers gently pressed against his flesh. He couldn't help remembering other places, other times, when those lovely hands had held and caressed him, made his body sing with pleasure. He became aroused and shifted uncomfortably in his seat. Annie might be determined to keep their relationship professional but Nick's mind—and body—were heading in a much more intimate direction. He forgot all about his fears of dependency and commitment as Annie continued to excite him with her touch.

"The swelling has gone down a little. Does it feel any better?" Annie looked up at him, and she did not fail to notice that he was obviously feeling much better.

"Nick . . ." she warned.

"I said before that you have great healing powers. I feel terrific." He reached down and caught her by the shoulders, pulling her toward him.

Annie struggled out of his grasp.

"You may be feeling terrific, mister, but your ankle is just hanging in." She strode across the room and removed two pills from the vial she'd placed on her table.

"For a doctor who's dead set against pills, you sure seem to know how to dish them out. How about some food instead? Or do you intend to mend my ankle and let me starve to death at the same time?"

"First take your medicine. Then I'll see what I can scrounge up in the fridge. I wasn't planning on a midnight meal."

Nick caught hold of her hand that still clasped the small white tablets. This time when he pulled her toward him she didn't resist. She landed on his lap, fitting perfectly. He held her close. She could feel his heart pounding against his chest. His fingers spun themselves around her rich, auburn strands. The feel, the texture, even the slightly apple scent of her shampoo was the same. He drew her face closer. Her eyes shone with a desire she couldn't mask. He held her gaze for a long moment and then he kissed her. Annie's lips parted, a sigh echoing her fleeing resistance.

"Oh, Annie," he whispered when he finally released her. "I want you so badly."

"It isn't enough, Nick." Annie had accepted his kiss, even returned it with equal passion, but it didn't alter anything. She never doubted Nick wanted her. But he wanted her in *his* way, on his terms.

"Annie, we both know that my tennis days aren't going to last forever." He smiled ironically. That had to be one of the biggest understatements of the year. "You always said that was what stood between us."

Annie got up. She looked down at the tablets still in her hand. They were beginning to melt because her palms were so moist. "Here, take these before they disintergrate completely."

79

He swallowed them mindlessly, his eyes fixed on her.

"I'll go find us some food." Her voice was muffled and strained.

Nick reached out for her again, but this time he didn't pull her to him. "I'm not hungry anymore," he said huskily. "Not for food, anyway."

Annie said nothing for a moment. Then she turned her head toward him. "You'll never be through with tennis, Nick. They'll have to carry you off the courts flat on your back before you quit. And even then, it will still be your mistress. When you can't woo her anymore you'll spend the rest of your life bemoaning her cruelty to you."

"Isn't that a little melodramatic?" he asked sarcastically.

"I don't hear you denying it," she said, then walked into the kitchen and put together a couple of sandwiches. She still had some roast beef in the fridge along with a half-finished bottle of wine.

She came back into the living room. Nick was stretched out on the couch.

"Here, eat your sandwich and then go sack out on my bed. I'll take the couch."

"No, this is fine," he said tightly. He winced as he sat back up and took a sandwich from Annie. She set a glass of ice water in front of him and poured a good portion of wine for herself.

"Hey, don't I get any of that?"

"You can't mix booze with pills," Annie said, taking a swallow. She sat down next to him on the couch, purposely putting a fair distance between them.

"You're cruel, Doc."

"I don't mean to be."

"Don't you?"

"What is that supposed to mean?" Annie's voice held a note of belligerance. Were they going to spend all of the next four months warring?

"I just wondered if you didn't take on this job to torment me." He smiled, but Annie heard the serious intent of his remark.

"So that's what I get for—for taking pity on your—your falling-apart body." She was starting to steam. All right, if he wanted war, she could do battle as well as the next guy. "If you remember correctly, Mister Wild Man Winters, you came begging me for help, not the other way around."

She expected Nick to counterattack. Her rage was totally deflated when he broke out into laughter.

"I should know better than to fight with a pro," he laughed. "Let's declare a truce. You are absolutely right. I came begging." His tone turned serious. "I do need you, Annie. At one time in my life I would have been too proud to say it. Besides, what could be more obvious?" He laughed again.

Annie felt a little dizzy. She put the glass of wine down. "Nick, what is it about you? Just when I think I've got you all figured out, you throw me another curve." She didn't know tears filled her eyes until Nick reached out and wiped a wayward tear drop off her cheek.

"I told you I've learned to be honest with you. Whatever happens, Annie, I intend to keep that promise."

"Do me a favor, don't promise me anything," Annie whispered. "I don't want to hold you to promises."

"It isn't a promise I made to you. I made it to myself exactly ten months and five days ago."

Annie shut her eyes. She, too, had kept track of the time. She hated doing it, hoping her need to count out the days would fade. Just as she hoped her need for Nick would disappear. When she opened her eyes again, she saw Nick watching her.

"Go to bed, Nick. I'm taking the couch," she said firmly.

"Tuck me in."

"No."

"I don't want to go to bed alone."

"I don't want to go to bed with you." Annie edged away from Nick.

"Yes, you do." Nick followed her.

"Nick, you're being adolescent," she said, her voice pleading.

"You always said I never really grew up." He slid his hands around her neck.

"I'll—I'll help you into my room. Then I'm going to go to bed on the couch," she repeated, more for herself than Nick this time.

"Thanks, Doc."

"Nick, I mean it."

He yawned. "You always were well meaning."

She knew he was intentionally leaning more of his weight on her than he needed to do as they crossed the room. She had to struggle to swing open the bedroom door. At least she had taken the cartons off of her bed this morning.

When she got him to the bed, he yawned again. "I can't figure out why I'm so tired. Come help me get my shirt off, will you?"

"Nick." Her voice was sounding like a broken record.

"Okay, okay." He stretched. "I'll manage."

As she turned away, he grabbed her hand. "Remember those fabulous backrubs you used to give me after a tough game?"

"That isn't part of the treatment tonight." She tried to release his grip, but this time he held on tight.

"Then, at least give me a purely professional kiss good-night," he said as he grinned, trying to fight back yet another yawn.

"You never stop trying, do you?" She sighed, smiling.

"Never." He was struggling to keep his eyes open. Somehow it was taking all his strength just to hold on to her hand. Then even that became impossible. He felt his hand slide off, falling heavily onto the bed.

"Hey, what were those pills, anyway?"

But Annie didn't bother answering that they were a much needed sedative. He was already asleep.

She bent down and gave him a brief, tender kiss, telling herself it was definitely a purely professional instinct.

Annie was awakened by a loud banging at her door.

"Movers."

She groaned, forgetting for a moment that she had spent a cramped, uncomfortable night on her couch. She almost fell off it as she turned over onto her back.

"Just a minute."

She struggled out of the tangled blankets and threw on her only unpacked bathrobe. It had seen better days. As she caught a glimpse of herself in the hall mirror, she realized so had she. It was hopeless to create any order out of her disheveled appearance. She opened the door to a large, burly man in a gray work-shirt, his sleeves carelessly rolled up, brilliantly colored tattoos proudly displayed on both of his thick-set arms.

"We got an early start," he announced. His eyes, after taking stock of the good-looking dame clutching her robe, surveyed the room.

"How many rooms you got here?" he mumbled.

"Three—well, four if you count the bathroom. Actually five, I guess, if I include the dining area." Her head was still muddled with sleepiness.

The mover looked at her as if she were a typical daffy dame. "Look, lady, the order lists three rooms, total."

"Then, why did you ask me how many rooms I had?" she snapped.

"Because sometimes the order goes out wrong. I got only one guy with me for this job, and if you got five rooms instead of the three you told us on the phone, I'm gonna have to get somebody else down here." He was none too happy. Neither was Annie.

"I tell you what. You call and get another man down here and while you're waiting for him, go have some coffee or something."

"Hey, lady, time is money. And it ain't my dough that's gonna be dished out while I hang around some coffee shop."

"Fine, fine. I understand." She reached into a bowl on the hall table and dished out a dime. "Here's money for the call. Don't worry. There's more where that came from," she said, her sarcasm completely eluding her target.

"Okay, lady. You're the boss. We'll be back in about thirty minutes." He threw the dime up in the air and caught it behind his back.

Annie had exactly a half hour to get showered, dressed, and see to her still-comatose patient in the bedroom. She slipped silently into the room and felt in her closet for her clothes. It wasn't too difficult even with the lights off, since almost everything was already packed.

"What was that, a Mickey Finn you slipped me last night?" Nick's voice came out slightly croaked. He rubbed his head and yawned.

85

"I had to do something about you." Annie grinned. "My powers can be mighty strong when necessary. Keep that in mind."

"Or else I could keep my mouth shut."

"An even better idea." She laughed.

"I meant only when you hand me some little white pills." He stretched, yawning again. "How about some coffee?"

"No time. In thirty minutes three big bruisers are going to descend on us, and I, for one, intend to be ready for them." She draped her clothes over a chair and walked over to the bed. "You can shower after me and then after I take care of the movers we can go back to your hotel and I'll help you get your things together. What time is the plane to Gstaad tonight?"

"Slow down, Doc. My head feels like a bowl of mush and you're moving a mile a minute. You always were a morning person."

"And you never could stand it." She pulled the covers off him. "Let me take a look at your ankle. How does it feel?"

"I don't know. Not even the top part of me is awake yet. My legs still haven't discovered it's time to get up."

Annie unrolled the bandage while he spoke. She paused to draw open the curtains.

Nick flinched against the glaring sun. "Ouch. My head feels worse than after a hangover. Even my hair is throbbing." Nick grinned at Annie, but she wasn't laughing back.

"Hey, that was a joke. Ha. Ha."

"Your head may be a joke," Annie answered

soberly, "but your ankle isn't any laughing matter."

Nick sat up. Now that his head was clearing he couldn't ignore the problem of his ankle. It not only felt pretty awful; it looked as though someone had inflated it with an air pump.

"It's going to be okay," Nick announced.

"That's supposed to be my line. And I'm not saying it. There is no way you are going to be fit to play in the Swiss Open, Nick. You have got to stay off your ankle for at least a few days."

"I don't start playing until the day after tomorrow."

"That's not going to be enough time for your ankle to handle the stress."

"Annie, be reasonable. If I don't enter the tournament on Tuesday, that's it for the whole week. I'm not going to lay on my duff waiting for the magic moment when you tell me it's time to play again. That could be next summer." Nick's features were hard.

"Now who's being unreasonable? What is the big deal about missing one lousy tournament? You swore you were going to cut back on the games if I took on your medical care." Annie's features were just as hard as Nick's. They were both winding up for a big battle.

"Annie, be my doctor, not my goddamn nursemaid. I've known this ankle of mine longer than you have. It's looked worse than this plenty of times before, but if I stay off it for a day I always manage to get it back in shape."

"Sure. And how many pain-killers do you take

from good old Bill Kenny so that you can 'manage'?"

"Annie, you are really pushing here. Let's cool it, okay?"

"Let's do more than that, Nick. Let's forget the whole damn thing. You don't need a doctor. You obviously have your own cures, and like you said, they work just great."

"There is nobody on earth that gets me as mad as you do, Annie. Not all the incompetent linesmen, umpires, cheating players. Will you stop being so stubborn! Why can't we work together? Compromise?"

"That's a beautiful word—compromise. I don't think you know what it means. The only way you compromise is by manipulating everyone to get your own way. Well, this is one"—she was about to say woman but switched it to—"doctor—that you are not going to get around. You either do it my way or count me out."

She grabbed her clothes and slammed the door to the bathroom before Nick had a chance to counterattack.

Later he limped into the kitchen to scout for some instant coffee. His head still felt puffy and the fight with Annie hadn't helped matters. Maybe she was right. Maybe this thing wasn't going to work out after all. He never had been good at taking orders.

But his ankle was killing him. Annie had been so mad she hadn't rewrapped the bandage and Nick had done a botched-up job of it. To top it off there wasn't any coffee to be found anywhere. He swallowed the remnants of some orange juice straight from the container and then tossed the empty carton into the trash.

The shower was going full force and he hoped Annie was letting off the rest of her steam in there. Now that he was fully awake, he figured they could probably iron things out. He wouldn't continue to argue. Instead, on Tuesday he would show her how good his ankle looked and she would go along with his plan.

The doorbell rang insistently. Nick limped over to it and let in the movers, three in all, similarly attired in gray work-shirts, the pockets all embossed with the words DUGGAN MOVERS.

"Ah, you must be Duggan," he said to all three with a laugh that was not returned. "Leave the bathroom for last, if you would, guys. The lady of the house is finishing her morning bath."

They shrugged and proceeded to ignore Nick as they trudged into the room. The guy in charge shouted gruff commands to the other two, telling them the order in which to move things in the living room. After he surveyed the other rooms, save for the bathroom per Nick's request, he came back into the living room and pitched in with the heavy pieces.

"Your wife doesn't count too well. I count three and a half rooms. There was no need for a third guy. You ought to know how easy she spends your money, buddy. This is gonna cost a third more than it should have."

"Ah, women." Nick feigned a sigh. "Aren't they all alike?"

This time he managed to get a smile out of the man from Duggan's.

The movers worked fast if a little sloppily. And Annie was taking one of the longest showers on record. Oh, well, maybe it was cooling her off.

Two of the movers hoisted up the desk, not seeing Annie's small black clutchbag in the corner. It tumbled to the ground, the contents spilling all over the place.

"That's okay, fellas, I'll take care of it." The movers merely grunted. Picking up purses wasn't part of their job.

Nick smiled as he started putting the items back in Annie's bag. It had always amazed him how Annie managed to fit so many things into one small space. Matchbook covers from a half dozen places, including one she'd picked up from dinner last night at Harborside which he pocketed for himself—he collected certain souvenirs, too—and a varied assortment of cosmetics, loose change, a very old and worn rabbit's foot, and a big enough collection of keys that probably unlocked every apartment Annie had ever lived in. He had difficulty getting her wallet to fit in the purse after cramming everything else back in.

He didn't spot the folded packet of papers on the floor until after he'd set Annie's purse on the windowsill. He bent down to retrieve what he first mistook for a pamphlet, meaning to prop it next to her purse. A familiar word caught his eye—Centurion. Nick unfolded the papers and looked at them more carefully. It was a contract from Centurion Enterprises. Puzzled, Nick skipped to the end of it. Annie's signature, that neat well-formed script, filled the bottom line.

Nick leaned against the wall and read it all, slowly and carefully. The generous salary, the fringe benefits, and the topper, a big, juicy donation to St. Mead's hospital in Dr. Ann Kneeland's name. Centurion sure knew how to take care of their people. And Annie sure knew how to negotiate a deal. Quite a bit of sugar to sweeten her difficult task. And he thought he was reading between the lines all this time. What an idiot. He had been reading the wrong book.

CHAPTER FIVE

Nick stared at the smoke rings Mac made with his cigar. Then he aimlessly looked around at the other tennis players scattered about the airport waiting room. Few people spoke, but for the most part it was a comfortable silence born out of months of being together on the pro circuit, and no longer finding it necessary to make small talk. Everyone was tired. It had been a long week in Delray Beach.

Nick focused for a moment on Jeff Reese and his wife, Barbara, sitting off by themselves at the end of the row of attached plastic seats. Their silence had nothing to do with comfort. Barbara was going along with the team to Gstaad. It was supposed to be a vacation break for her, before returning to teach summer-school classes. Only she sure didn't look in a holiday mood. Neither did Jeff. Nick couldn't decide which of the two he felt sorrier for. Both, he concluded.

Then again, Nick was ripe for feeling sorry for people at this moment. And he put himself at the top of the list. Annie had played him for a fool and he was boiling mad. And depressed. He kept telling himself he wanted Annie to show up so that he could have the pleasure of telling her off.

Annie Kneeland, the woman of such fine principles, the shining example of honesty and integrity. What a laugh. She was as much a commodity as she had accused him of being. She had let herself be bought off as willingly as Nick.

He had played back dozens of arguments in his head all day long, but they didn't relieve his anger or frustration. He needed Annie for that.

The plane was taking off in less than forty minutes. For international flights most passengers showed up at least an hour early. Annie was late. Nick kept trying not to watch the large clock on the wall. Every minute that passed added to the possibility that she wasn't planning on showing up at all.

Nick kept telling himself Annie wouldn't turn down the terrific deal she'd made—not because of an argument of so little consequence.

Annie had not cooled off in her shower that morning. By the time she stepped out of the bathroom, she had come up with several more things she wanted to throw at Nick. But he wasn't there.

The movers were just about finished. And when she asked them about Nick, they said they didn't know where he had gone. One of them did say he looked kind of mad when he had left, but he hadn't left a message for her.

Annie had no idea that Nick had read her

contract with Centurion. Even when she saw it next to her purse, propped up against the windowsill, she assumed one of the movers had tossed both items there.

She interpreted Nick's walking out as his way of telling her he was going to ignore her medical advice. So that's it, she decided. She was going to have her vacation after all. Of course there was the matter of the contract. Annie had no doubt Centurion would bring suit against her if she reneged on the deal. But she had a good argument. You can't treat someone medically if he refuses treatment. And Nick had clearly spelled out his refusal.

She looked around the empty, barren room and a wave of depression washed over her. She didn't even have a chair to curl into and have a good cry. Instead she grabbed the contract and tossed it across the room. Not even the staples came undone. It was still intact. She picked it up. Leaning against the wall, just as Nick had done fifteen minutes ago, she reread it.

Contracts always sounded officially binding, but this one seemed even more so. She could just picture the gleeful look on Grimes's face as he went after her in court.

There was also the hefty donation to St. Mead's to consider. Annie had told Grimes she wouldn't be bribed, but now that the money was already slated for the hospital Annie had a hard time justifying its withdrawal.

For most of the rest of the day she managed not to think about where Nick fit in. She dropped off the key at her landlord's apartment, had a last lunch with Paula at one of their favorite restaurants, made a few calls, and took a long walk on the beach. She had thought she'd worked out all the reasons why she was going to have to show up at that airport tonight. Yet something kept getting in the way.

She was running out of time and rationalizations. Either she was going to keep her commitment and work things out with Nick or she was going to call back that resort in Palm Beach and see if they could reinstate her canceled reservation. She rarely had felt so immobile and indecisive. The way the minute hand was sweeping away the hours, Annie was going to have to make up her mind pretty soon.

Getting in the taxi, she finally focused on the deepest reason she had told the cabbie to get her to the airport—and to step on it or she'd miss the plane to Switzerland. She could not desert Nick. He needed her. He was probably going to fight it to the bitter end, but they both knew the truth. It was also true that right now Annie needed Nick. At least she needed this time together to sort out unfinished business.

There was something else. Nick had said it himself. He had changed. Annie remembered she had thought that had been true last year, too. But this time she sensed the change in a deeper, more profound way. She wasn't certain what it meant or how it would affect the two of them and she was not even sure she was seeing things clearly. Maybe the next few months would put it all in focus.

After checking in her bags at the terminal, she still had nearly a half hour. She walked briskly down the long corridor, her high heels clicking rhythmically, echoing through the windowless chamber. Annie wore a simple rose-colored blouse and a matching print skirt. A casual cotton jacket in a paler shade of pink was draped over her arm. Her pocketbook, this one a tote style large enough to hold all of her paraphernalia, was slung over her shoulder. She made a pretty picture and a number of men walking along that airport corridor were quick to take notice of the strikingly attractive woman with a flare for color and style. Annie was too busy preparing herself for her next confrontation with Nick to notice the approving glances.

The confrontation was postponed. When Annie arrived at Gate Eleven, several of the tennis players spotted her. Annie knew quite a few of them from her days on the circuit and she smiled as people started coming over to her. Apparently few people were informed of Annie's position on the team and she was bombarded with questions.

Jeff Reese gave her a friendly bear hug. Barbara didn't move from her seat.

"So you really tied the knot," Annie teased. "How about introducing me to your wife?"

Jeff waved to Barbara, who reluctantly rose and walked over. Annie was taken aback by the woman's icy greeting. Things must really be going terribly for Jeff's wife not to even manage reasonable civility.

Mac came up from behind and squeezed her shoulder affectionately.

"Glad to see you finally made it. Our boy hasn't been looking any too good. He wouldn't let anyone take a peek at that ankle, either. Guess he only wants his personal physician to tend to him."

Annie followed Mac's gaze over to Nick—a very sullen, distant Nick who was busy studying a nearly full ashtray beside him.

Mac gently shoved her in Nick's direction.

"See if you can cheer him up," he said, patting her on the back.

Annie could have told Mac that she was probably the last person in the world who could cheer Nick up, but she kept the information to herself. It was difficult enough in a group like this to maintain any privacy. She was not about to offer up anything for gossip. There would be enough of that anyway.

She sat down beside Nick. He didn't move a muscle.

"I guess we are still at war," she said quietly, keeping her own features intentionally bland.

Nick didn't answer.

"I almost didn't show up," she went on in that same quiet tone.

Nick finally looked over at her. "Oh, I was sure you would decide it was worth it to hang in." He gave her a long, hard look.

"What does that mean?" she retorted, forgetting to keep her voice down. A couple of heads turned. Annie didn't notice.

"You're smart. Figure it out."

Annie had no idea what he was talking about, but she did know that somehow the channels had gotten changed since this morning and Nick was definitely in a new battle. And Annie hadn't yet figured out the story line.

She was getting nowhere fast and she decided this was not the ideal spot for starting new fights.

"How does your ankle feel?" She tried to keep the edge out of her voice.

"Your concern is touching, Doc."

"And your sarcasm is infuriating," Annie retorted. "Could we take a walk and talk in private about what's going on?" This was getting ridiculous and Annie was reaching the end of her fuse.

"I'm not walking very well these days and I don't much feel like chatting. Why don't we accept the reality of this situation? You do your job and I'll do mine. If we play our cards right we'll both come out ahead." He picked up a magazine from the empty chair beside him and started reading.

"And I accused you of being adolescent. You're absolutely infantile, Nick Winters. And if you want to behave like a child I'll start treating you as one." What she really felt like doing was grabbing that magazine from his hands and forcing him to talk. She probably would have, if there weren't suddenly a commotion a little way down the aisle.

Annie looked up to see Barbara Reese fleeing down the hall, looking as white as a ghost, and Jeff rushing after her. Mac hurried over to Annie.

"Something's wrong with Barbara. I was sitting there talking to her when all of a sudden she turns ash-gray and slumps in her seat. She only passed out for a second, but she mumbled something about feeling awful and took off for the ladies' room."

Annie was already moving toward the ladies' room as Mac finished his account, his pace keeping up with hers. She didn't notice that Nick was following.

Annie met up with Jeff at the door. He was about to enter when Annie grabbed him.

"Take it easy, Jeff. I don't think the rest of the women in there would appreciate your popping in. I'll see to Barbara. You wait out here."

A little color had come back to Barbara's face. She was sitting on a stool, slightly bent over.

Annie wet a strip of toweling, rolled it up, and pressed it on Barbara's forehead. Barbara was still pale and shaky but she managed a hostile glance at Annie and pulled the cloth off her head.

"I'm just trying to help," Annie said with a note of irritation. What was with this woman, anyway? They had never met before and yet Barbara was behaving as though they were already enemies.

"Leave me alone. I'm fine. Probably something I ate." Barbara was still feeling dizzy, and as much as she would have liked to get up and stomp out of the room, she had to keep her hands clamped to the edges of the stool for balance.

"I don't get it," Annie said with more curiosity than annoyance. "What exactly is your gripe with me?"

Barbara looked up at her. Some of the coldness had dissipated, her face reflecting a disconcerting look of helplessness and sadness. "It's not what you've done; it's what you more than likely will do."

Annie shook her head in confusion. "Has everyone on this tour learned some new kind of language that I don't know? People are talking in circles, alluding to God knows what, and I am getting damn tired of it. Look, would you please give me some good old straight talk? What exactly am I likely to do?"

"Go to bed with my husband."

Well, Barbara couldn't be straighter than that, and Annie couldn't have been more shocked.

"What? Are you crazy, Barbara? Why would I go to bed with Jeff?" She was too astounded to sound angry or insulted.

"Why should you be any different from the others? He's probably taken every one of the women players to bed, so you come along as the new challenge." Barbara was feeling less dizzy, allowing her anger to resurface with its full force.

"I'm not in any position to talk for Jeff or know anything about his sexual conquests, but I will tell you one thing I do know for certain. I am not going to bed with your husband. Firstly, I don't go around sleeping with married men. Secondly, Jeff is not my type. And thirdly"—Annie shook her finger at Barbara—"thirdly, what is the matter with you?"

"I'm pregnant."

Barbara sure knew how to throw zingers. Annie stood there with her mouth open.

Barbara wasn't finished yet. "Jeff doesn't know."

Annie pulled up a stool beside the distraught woman, who had dropped her head into her hands. "I don't think we can make it. And I don't know what to do."

Annie let Barbara have her cry and then, handing her a tissue from her tote bag, she asked, "Are you so sure Jeff is fooling around? You were dead wrong about me, you know. Maybe you're wrong about the others, too."

Barbara wiped her eyes. She made an effort to smile. When her features softened, Annie saw that Jeff's wife was a very attractive woman. Her dark eyes, jet-black hair, and tawny skin gave her an exotic earthiness. Her smile lighted up her face and gave her a warmth that was both appealing and soft. Annie could see why Jeff had chosen her.

"I guess you think I'm a jealous shrew," Barbara said, her smile fading.

"Pregnant women are often more emotional than usual," Annie offered.

Barbara smiled again. "I'm Italian. I come from a long line of emotional women."

Annie grinned. She was getting to like this lady.

"My jealousy doesn't come from thin air." Barbara hesitated. She found herself liking Annie. "Jeff has been unfaithful." Again she paused, casting her eyes down to the white tiled floor. "He confessed. So you see"—she looked back over to Annie—"I do have some justification."

Annie didn't know what to say. She did wonder why Barbara had stuck it out if what she said was true, but it wasn't her business to ask.

As it turned out, Barbara provided the answer anyway. "I love him," she said earnestly. "And what makes it so damn frustrating is that I really think Jeff loves me. He has sworn to me a hundred times since the whole thing happened last spring that there has never been another incident." She gave Annie one of her pained smiles. "I want to believe him. I want this marriage to work, but how can it survive given everything that happened?"

Annie knew she should mind her own business. On the other hand she couldn't ignore Barbara's distress. Despite Nick's accusations she usually had a very comforting bedside manner. And Barbara was in a lot of pain.

"Did this relationship Jeff had go on for a long time?" Annie asked. She still couldn't imagine Jeff carrying on a lengthy affair only months after he'd gotten married.

"Oh, no," Barbara said without hesitation. "It was only one time. If—if it had gone on, I wouldn't be sitting here in this predicament right now."

"Can I tell you how I would diagnose the situation?" Annie asked softly.

Barbara nodded.

"I think Jeff was taking a last fling, a kind of final grasp at something he thought was going to be hard to give up. Don't you think, Barbara, if he was able to tell you about it, it means something important?" Maybe, Annie thought to herself, if Nick had been able to talk honestly about his relationship with Lynn, before rather than after her discovery, they would have had a future. She forced her mind back to the present problem.

"I think that way some of the time," Barbara admitted. "But every time I see him looking at another woman or going off alone with some sexy tennis stars, never mind the groupies that hover around, I start thinking how easy it would be for Jeff to slip again. When I saw him sweep you in his arms tonight, I—I saw red. You're gorgeous, single, and you're going to be in close contact with Jeff while I'm knitting booties back home."

Annie took Barbara's hand. "Well, you never have to worry about me, so you can knit those booties without a care. I'll also keep an eye on Jeff, but to be honest with you, I doubt he needs watching by me or you."

"No. You don't have to watch Jeff. If anything is going to happen, all the watching in the world wouldn't matter. Besides I feel guilty enough burdening you with my problems. Knowing Nick like I do, I think you've probably got enough of your own worries."

"What do you know about Nick and me?" Annie asked straightforwardly.

"I know you're his doctor," Barbara said with a sympathetic smile, "and I know that the two of you were, well—pretty serious for a time last year."

"I guess you know the whole story. I am only his doctor now," Annie confirmed, but she could tell from the look Barbara gave her that she wasn't all that convincing.

"I feel a little sorry for you," Barbara said.

Annie looked up sharply. She certainly wasn't trying to engender sympathy.

"I mean, having a patient like Nick to cope with," Barbara explained quickly, understanding Annie's expression.

"You're right," Annie said with a laugh. The laugh died quickly when she thought about Nick's sullen mood.

Barbara stood up. Annie quickly followed suit.

"Are you all right now?" Annie asked with concern. "I assume that spell was related to the pregnancy."

"I'm fine. And I'm lucky it doesn't happen too often or Jeff might get suspicious."

"Barbara, you're going to have to tell him sometime soon. How do you plan to explain the maternity clothes?"

"I know. I know." Barbara nodded. "It's just that I don't want to use the baby as the reason Jeff and I stay together." She gave Annie a warm hug. "Thanks—for everything." They started toward the door.

Jeff was pacing back and forth in front of the ladies' room. He turned abruptly as it opened.

"Honey, are you okay?" To Annie, he said, "Barbara's never been sick the whole time I've known her. She's certainly never passed out."

"Relax, Jeff. Barbara's fine." She smiled at them both.

"Just something I ate," Barbara told him quickly. Not that she thought Annie would give away any secrets, but she still had not sorted things out enough to tell Jeff the truth or start making him curious.

"Right," Annie confirmed. "Why don't you take her over to the snack bar for a quick cup of tea? We should be boarding in less than fifteen minutes."

Jeff put his arm around his wife and gently led her down the corridor.

"Well, you certainly won Barbara over."

Annie hadn't noticed Nick leaning against the wall.

"She's a real nice lady," Annie said cautiously. Nick looked a little less hostile, but she wasn't taking any chances.

"Why did you show up, Annie?"

"A commitment is a commitment. I agreed to get you through the next four months and I'm going to try to keep up my side of the agreement."

"Of course you will. You've got quite a bit riding on it. You'll stick it out," he said cynically.

"Nick, are we going to continue talking in two different languages? What exactly are you so all-fired mad about?" The hallway was far from empty, but Annie was too irritated to care.

"Who was it? Grimes or McCafferty? Probably Grimes. He's the more generous of the two. Yes, and he sure was generous with you, wasn't he, Annie? For a minute there you had me believing . . ."

Annie wasn't sure at first how much of her reaction was due to her own anger and how much was a self-protective maneuver. What she did know was that it was safer for Nick to believe she had come along on this ride for the money rather than for the deeper feelings that Nick had begun to revive. He was definitely beginning to believe more than was safe—for her.

"I gather you found the contract."

"It made mighty interesting reading. Literally kept me on the edge of my seat."

"Look, Nick, I'm sorry if your feelings are hurt. Or maybe it's only your pride. I didn't lie to you about my concern for your health, but I also have no qualms about getting well paid for my services. I told you right along this was a professional arrangement only."

"I get the message loud and clear," Nick snapped back. "Maybe if you get around to it, after tending to my ankle you can look at my head. I certainly need it examined."

Annie watched him stomp off. She'd seen him do that dozens of times on the tennis courts. He may have grown up in some ways, but Nick was still adept at pulling off a tantrum. Annie had to smile despite it all.

They were beginning to embark when Annie got back to Gate Eleven. Nick was in line, handing in his ticket. Annie fell in behind the others.

The 747 was full. Summer tourists occupied the majority of seats, but the tennis group took up quite a chunk in the rear of the plane. Annie checked her seat number. Of course it would be next to Nick. Mac had arranged her passage and assumed she would want to sit next to her patient.

Nick sat with his eyes closed in the middle seat of a triple. There was no way to avoid him by even one space. She recognized Stanislas Vostek sitting on the other side of Nick. Annie didn't know the player personally, but she did know he spoke little English.

Vostek greeted Annie with a warm, friendly smile as she got settled in her seat. He offered to get up and put her large tote bag in the overhead compartment. Before Annie got her message across that she preferred to keep the bag with her, Vostek had begun to rise. In the process he also accidentally brushed against Nick's ankle. Nick let out an involuntary groan. Vostek apologized profusely in his thick Yugoslavian accent, Nick nodding that it was okay.

"That bad, huh?" Annie reached into her tote for a small medicine bag and snapped it open. She signaled for the flight attendant and asked for some water.

"Forget it. I don't want any of your little white wonders. I don't need any help sleeping, thank you," Nick grumbled, forcing himself not to show the pain Stan's kick had wrought.

"If you thought my bedside manner was terrible before, you haven't seen anything yet. Shall I tell you what I do with stubborn patients who won't take their medicine?" Annie hissed.

Nick laughed through his pain and anger. "I feel sorry for those kids at St. Mead's. They have no idea what they're going to be in for."

"I doubt that the worst of those kids will be as impossible as you. Now are you going to take your medicine or am I going to ask our friend next to us to hold you down while I hold your nose and force those pills down your throat?"

"Where did you learn to be so vicious?" Nick taunted. "Boy, if you'd had some of that on the tennis court you would have been number one."

"I guess some of us lack that killer instinct when we play games." Annie was not going to let Nick get to her. She reminded herself that Nick's anger was also her protection.

"Some of us play to win and others always play

it safe," Nick answered, gazing into those blue eyes of hers; trying to figure out what was behind them. Annie has changed, too, he thought, aware of a new pain—this one in his gut. He took the pills from her outstretched palm and swallowed them without another word.

CHAPTER SIX

The plane landed in Geneva, Switzerland, at eight in the morning, Swiss time. Everyone was a little bleary eyed as they disembarked. Fortunately the chartered bus that would drive them the hour and a half to Gstaad was outside waiting for them.

Luggage and tennis gear were stowed in the baggage compartment, several of the players taking their favorite or special rackets on the bus with them. Those rackets had too much value to be thrown into storage.

Annie had wrapped Nick's ankle shortly before they got off the plane. She noticed that the swelling had gone down a little and she had already worked out in her mind the regimen for the next couple of days. She was still convinced that Nick's ankle would not be strong enough to withstand the grueling week of the Swiss Open, but she also knew that this was an important event. If there was some way she could get him in shape she was going to do it. However, Annie kept that thought to herself. If, in her medical opinion, he shouldn't play, Annie was going to be insistent that he cancel out.

Nick slid into a seat beside Kathy Mills. For having had only a couple of hours' sleep (those pills had been anti-inflammatories rather than sedatives) Nick managed to be unusually affable. Kathy, in her mid-thirties, was one of the old pros. Nick liked her. They had a friendly, uncomplicated relationship and right now Nick was looking for just that. The tediously long flight beside Annie had not been easy. At one point Annie had fallen asleep, her head tumbling accidentally on to his shoulder. His first impulse had been to put his arm around her and draw her closer, but the thought alone provoked too many ambivalent feelings. So he sat perfectly still, and when Annie shifted in her sleep, her head falling away from him, Nick suffered the loss in silence.

Kathy was exhausted, but she tried to respond to Nick's conversation between yawns. Every now and then her eyes traveled over to Annie, who sat up front next to Mac. Kathy noticed that Annie, too, was strikingly animated following such a long, uncomfortable night flight. It was amazing how nervous energy could keep people going.

Kathy knew about Nick and Annie. She had also been around when Nick and Lynn Carey were making the scene. It was a good thing Lynn was off on her honeymoon with Greg Altman. Things were going to be hot enough on this tour without a triangle to complicate matters more.

"I hear the Council is really getting ready to clamp down," Nick was saying.

Kathy stifled another yawn. "It's ridiculous. Oh, I know there are a few players who take some extra money under the table to appear at a couple of the tournaments, but I think Stringer and his cronies are pushing it too far."

"They're not only digging out who's taking guarantee money. The rumor is they suspect quite a few players of splitting prize money and purposely losing certain matches. Those are mighty heavy charges. It could mean hefty fines, even suspensions," Nick said hotly. Ever since the Pro Tennis Council had gotten on this kick to ferret out wrongdoers, tensions had begun to run high among the players. Everyone was wondering who the bad guys were, casting suspicious glances every now and then, nervously concerned about being unjustly accused. This kind of thing could ruin careers.

Nick disapproved of the way the Council was handling things. If they had charges to bring out against someone, then they ought to get on with it. They had been on this thing for months and Nick was beginning to think it was a setup. It seemed to him the Council was getting nowhere fast with their investigation, so they were throwing rumors all over the place hoping that some of the players would get nervous and slip up.

"Well, my conscience is clear," Kathy said, stretching. "So I can sleep easy. Which is really what I want to do, pal. Why don't you try to do the same?" Kathy stretched. She still had an hour to get some sleep and she could see this conversation was only serving to get Nick more riled up.

Mac was having similar thoughts about Annie, who had been talking nonstop since they boarded the bus. At least he didn't have to say much. Annie was handling the conversation for both of them. He leaned back in his seat, chewed on his unlit cigar, and let Annie ramble on. She had just finished a discourse on her work at the Sports Medicine Center and she was rolling into a detailed description of her medical plans for Nick.

"The thing is, Mac," Annie said earnestly, "I'm going to need you to back me. Your interests and mine could conceivably clash."

Mac didn't bother removing the cigar from his mouth as he mumbled, "I don't look for problems, Doc. You take care of Nick and put him on his feet and I'll back you all the way."

"Good, Mac." Annie smiled. "Because if Nick's ankle doesn't look a hell of a lot better by tomorrow afternoon, you are going to be missing one player for the Swiss Open."

Mac removed the cigar. "Doc, that would be real bad for Nick. The Swiss Open isn't some little backwater tournament. I'm banking on you to help get him in shape for it. That is why you're here, isn't it?"

Annie knew there were going to be problems. Mac was overestimating the realities of medical

113

science. He was also probably overestimating Nick's stamina under physical stress. Mac may have witnessed a few losing matches when Nick was in bad shape, but he'd also seen Nick play some of his finest games under a great deal of pain. Annie let the conversation drop. She didn't feel like talking anymore.

Mac's reaction hadn't come as a surprise. She knew he cared about Nick, but Mac also wanted him out there playing. Annie was beginning to realize that she could easily become cast as the villain in this piece unless she managed to work some medical miracles. If not, there was going to be no one on her side—especially not Nick.

Annie knocked lightly on Nick's door. She had slept for almost two hours and had then taken a quick tour of the hotel facilities she was going to need for Nick's treatment. She was pleased to find not only steaming-hot whirlpool baths, indoor and outdoor swimming pools, but also an exercise room outfitted with the most modern equipment around. In fact, the setup was nearly as good as the Fisher Center back in Florida. Annie felt her spirits lifting. If she was going to try for miracles at least she had all the necessary ingredients at her fingertips. She signed up for private hours for the whirlpool and exercise room and picked up a couple of sandwiches for her and Nick.

Nick didn't hear her first knock. He tried to ignore the second one. He was in the middle of a great dream. The third rap was more insistent and he gave in.

"Good morning, or rather good afternoon," Annie said, checking her watch. It was a few minutes to twelve. "We've got a busy day ahead of us, Winters, so rise and shine."

"Do you have to be so cheery every time I wake up?" he grumbled. And look so damn good, he added silently. He reached for his bathrobe.

"Forget the robe. Throw on your swim trunks and a running suit. Here," she said, tossing him a turkey sandwich wrapped in wax paper, "eat this while you get ready."

"No sleep, meals thrown at me, a drill instructor eagerly biting at the bit to put me through some kind of living torture. What are you trying to do to me?"

"I am trying to get you on your feet. So get moving." Annie opened Nick's suitcase and began rummaging for his clothes.

"Do you mind? Last I remember you were adamant about not helping me to undress. I can dress myself as well."

"Fine, fine. I'll meet you down at the gym. It's in the basement," Annie said, moving away from the suitcase. "You never used to be this grumpy when you woke up." Before he had a chance to answer, she swept out of the room.

Nick met her downstairs ten minutes later. He took a couple of bites of the sandwich in the elevator, tossing the rest away outside the exercise room. Annie was busy setting up some of the equipment when he walked in.

"Do we have this place to ourselves?" he asked.

"For an hour. I didn't want anyone to hear the screams as I tortured you," Annie teased.

Nick looked around the room. Some athletes really went for rigorous workouts in a big way. Others put themselves through the paces only because it was a necessary part of the job. Nick belonged to the latter group. He often thought that one of the few advantages to retiring would be saying good-bye to barbells, weights, and pulleys.

"Are you sure about this? Maybe I ought to stay off my feet and keep the old ankle up on a pillow."

"I'm the one getting paid to be the doctor," Annie said, without thinking.

"So you are."

The hostile tone in Nick's voice again reminded Annie how sore a point this was for Nick. She felt a flicker of temptation to tell him the whole truth. Instead, she finished adjusting the weights.

Nick took his place at the machine, swinging both ankles under the bar.

"Now, take it easy the first few times. If you feel too much strain, don't get macho on me and try to stick with it," Annie ordered.

"What do you want from me, Annie? First you tell me I'm adolescent, then infantile, and now you warn me not to be macho. You also didn't seem to like it when I acted like a man," he pointed out, his tone turning seductive. "There doesn't seem to be any way to please you these days."

"It would please me if—if—" she was having trouble getting the words out. Nick's hooded gaze was disconcerting, as were the thoughts springing into her mind.

Nick pulled Annie to him, the thin metal bar pressing against her calves.

"Tell me what you want," he whispered in her ear, his voice insistent.

The words reverberated through her body, arousing her, making her lose her grip on the promises and warnings that she'd been working so hard at building.

"Don't complicate things," she whispered back, pleading.

"They couldn't be more complicated." He kissed her, pulling back the moment she began to respond. "See what I mean?"

She could feel the heat rising to her face. She could also feel the sensations Nick's caressing hands were generating inside of her. The professional relationship she had been so insistent upon was fast slipping out the window.

Nick fixed his gaze on her. "Is this all part of the contract, too? I've been lousy lately at reading between the lines, so I might have missed the part where you're supposed to go to any lengths to get my cooperation."

Annie flinched. If he hadn't been holding on to her wrists she would have slapped him.

117

"My biggest regret is that I didn't throw Grimes out of my office, the way I wanted to. I foolishly let myself care too much," she said scornfully.

"About your poor underprivileged kids and that dilapidated hospital?" he shouted.

"About *you,* you damn idiot! I cared too much about you," she said as she pulled herself away from him. "Grimes told me they were going to drown you in pain-killers to get you through the season. He couldn't care less if you ended up crippled for life as long as he got you through all your contract commitments." She paused for breath, aware that she was shouting through her tears and not giving a damn. She turned on him. "I didn't want to see you destroyed. I didn't want to let them take every last piece of you, chew you up, and then spit you out when they find themselves a new young superstar. But maybe that's okay with you. When you asked for my help I was foolish enough to believe you would take it. But you want the same thing Grimes, Mac, and all those eager fans out there want. You want to believe you're indestructible and you want me to make sure you stay that way."

She started for the door, but Nick reached her before she got there.

"Leave me alone, Nick. I can't play the game your way. Go sue me."

Nick held her by the shoulders. She started to struggle and then gave it up.

"Annie, I'm sorry." He cupped her chin as she tried to look away. "I'm sorry for a lot of things."

"It isn't going to work, Nick."

"Yes, it is. Because you're right. And because I really don't want to spend my retirement being pushed around in a wheelchair."

Annie looked up into his eyes. "If you play on that ankle tomorrow, you very well might have to reserve that chair."

"I hear you, Doc." He smiled, touching her cheek with a tender stroke. "How about if I go through your paces and you suspend judgment until tomorrow morning? If you still think I shouldn't play then, I won't."

Annie cocked her head to one side, her gaze suspicious. "Do you really mean it?"

"Scout's honor."

"Okay, I'll accept the compromise. So, let's get to work."

Nick gripped her elbow. "You never did answer me."

Annie looked puzzled.

"About what you really wanted," he said, smiling slowly.

"No, I never did," she answered. "I want us to get along. And don't go reading between any more lines." She took his hand and led him back to the exercise machine. "Now, quit procrastinating. I know how you hate working out."

Nick laughed. It was a rich, warm, earthy laugh, free of anger and suspicion. It sounded good to both of them. Nick faced his exercises with new optimism.

An hour later he was less optimistic and aching from head to toe. He was ready to cry for mercy. And she was worried about him being macho!

"Stop groaning, Nick," Annie cajoled. "If we don't strengthen the other muscles in your leg, all the pressure is going to keep going to that ankle."

"When's recess?" he muttered.

"In a few minutes. And after a good rubdown you can relax in a whirlpool."

"Now, that's the best thing you've said all morning."

Annie was true to her word. Ten minutes later, after a refreshing hot shower, Nick, with a white hotel towel around his waist, stretched himself out on the black leather massage table. As Annie walked over to him, rolling up the sleeves of her cotton blouse, Nick smiled.

"Brings back memories, doesn't it?"

"Let's concentrate on the present," Annie said defensively. "Maybe I ought to see if one of the trainers is around to give you a rubdown."

"Scared?" he challenged. "Come on, Annie, where's that terrific professional distance?"

Annie dug her fingers into his calf.

"Ouch." He laughed. "I should know better than to challenge you."

"That's right, Winters. I've been told by some people that I can be really vicious."

"You work kindly on my aching muscles and I'll work on my big mouth." Nick grinned.

The casual banter did not erase the memories

for either of them. Annie remembered all those sensual massages; the feel of Nick's body growing aroused beneath her fingertips, the look in his eyes as she gently but firmly unknit all the tension and tightness in his muscles, the hunger that was generated between them as he invariably pulled her to him and began his own erotic strokes.

Nick closed his eyes. Her touch held the same magic. And generated the same longing. He made no effort to fight the feeling. Nor did his body. Unless Annie was doing this massage with her eyes closed, she knew damn well just how much he wanted her. He opened his eyes to see her reaction.

"Turn over," she ordered briskly, praying that her face wasn't flushed.

Nick burst out laughing. He sat up and took hold of her hands. "That could be a painful experience."

"Nick, you're impossible. I'm trying hard to . . ."

"I know how hard you're trying," he said softly. "I'm impressed."

"Let's skip the rest of the rubdown. I'll go check on the whirlpool."

Nick followed her across the hall. Annie had reserved the whirlpool for two o'clock. She walked into the well-heated room to make sure it was empty. Nick came in behind her.

"It's all yours," Annie said to him. "Do some of those isometrics while you're in the water and don't stay in too long."

"I think you better prompt me, Doc. I have a hard time remembering exactly what to do." He looked at her, grinning.

"Oh, I think you remember what to do," Annie answered with a throaty laugh.

"Refresh my memory." He swept her up in his arms and headed for the whirlpool.

"Nick, let go of me. You're crazy. I don't even have a bathing suit on," she protested, trying to get down.

"Neither do I." He grinned.

He was at the edge of the water. His towel had easily given way in the struggle. He took one step in.

"This isn't funny," Annie warned.

"You've been in charge for the last two hours. Now it's my turn."

"Nick!" The next moment she was underwater. "You idiot," she gasped, catching her breath. "Look at me. I'm—I'm . . ."

"You're all wet." He grinned. "Look's like I'm going to have to do some doctoring after all. Wouldn't want you to catch cold with those drenched clothes on."

"In hundred-degree water?" Annie quipped, stepping back against the edge of the Jacuzzi as Nick pursued her.

He smirked as he started tugging her blouse out of her gym pants. Annie caught hold of his hands.

"This won't change anything," she insisted.

"Oh, yes, it will. It's going to make us both feel

a hell of a lot better," he whispered as he started to unbutton her shirt.

"For now. Only for now." Her voice lacked conviction. Nick was nibbling on her ear while his hands tugged off her soaked shirt.

"We both decided to stick to the here and now," he reminded her before capturing her lips, stifling all further protests.

He had Annie's cooperation as he stripped off the rest of her wet clothes. The hot foamy water swirled around them both as Nick pushed the wet strands of her hair from her face, then swept her into his arms. Her slender legs draped naturally around his hips, her arms encircling his neck.

Nick's lips moved to the slender curve of her neck as Annie pressed more tightly against him, their hot bodies searing each other with an ever-growing need.

Clinging to each other, their hands exploring places they well remembered, they both sensed something new, something at once more savage and more urgent. The months apart had stoked their hunger to a level that neither of them had been aware of. There was a new dimension, one no longer possible for them to fight.

Now. Now, Annie told herself. Now is all there is. "I want you so much, Nick." The words came easily, her desire pushing everything else from her mind. The erotic movements of his hands down her back, over her firm buttocks, made her head spin. The warm whirlpool added to her light-headedness. Nick lifted her up in his arms and carried her out of the water. He laid her on one of the soft, cushioned mats set out for the guests to rest on. He fell beside her, his eyes taking in every detail, every marvelous curve and line. The water had left her body glistening, her ivory skin almost translucent. Nick had always found her beautiful, but never so much as now. He watched her breasts rise and fall with each quickened breath. He gazed into her sea-blue eyes filled with the desire he had longed to see again.

His hand trembled as he reached out to stroke her breasts. Annie ran her fingers through his hair as Nick bent his head, cupping her breasts with his hands, his lips and tongue trailing from one to another. She laughed. His mustache always tickled—in a way she loved. Intentionally, he glided his upper lip against her flesh in a feathery sweep.

Annie arched her back as Nick's lips brushed intimately down her belly. Her hands dug into the strongly defined muscles of his shoulders, her lips half-parted in quivering delight. They had begun to dry off, but the warmth their bodies had captured from the Jacuzzi had only grown more heated. As Annie ran her hands down his spine, Nick's skin felt fiery. She slid her hands onto his hard buttocks, pressing him more tightly to her with passionate force, her hips grinding against him. Nick sought out her lips once more, capturing Annie's throaty moan, kissing her now with an urgency she avidly returned. When he released her lips, her moan escaped into the air. Nick buried his face in her hair, the hinted scent of apples tingling his nostrils.

Wherever he touched her now evoked quivering, urgent sensations. She clutched him tighter, her legs parting to receive him, her body joyfully responding to his deep, penetrating thrusts. She wrapped her legs around him, moving with him in a rhythm they knew so well.

Annie's body began to burn. She was on fire, about to burst into a million pieces. Blazing, sparkling colors swirled inside of her like the jets of the whirlpool, her cries echoing against the cool tile walls of the small room. And then, at the very moment she was certain she could bear it no longer, the explosion erupted, scattering a rainbow of fiery colors around them both. It was a feeling of such utter abandon and ecstasy that Annie clutched Nick even tighter to keep from floating off.

Nick held on just as tightly, his own body feeling as though it could as easily drift away.

"Oh, Annie," he murmured breathlessly, as he tenderly stroked her cheek. "You've taken all the pain away." He smiled as his hands gently moved to her arms, then the exquisite curve of her hips. "I feel like a new man."

Annie smiled. "So that's what it takes to cure you."

"Yup. See all the time we wasted on those dumb machines."

"Oh, no, Winters. I may have deviated from the regimen for a crazy moment, but those machines are going to be a big part of your life for the next few months." Annie sat up.

"So are you." He tried to push her back down, wanting her once more.

But Annie resisted. Nick let his mustache brush along her shoulders as he planted tiny kisses along her still-warm skin.

"For the next few months," Annie added, trying to ignore the tantalizing touch of his lips. Nick's fingers swept away her damp hair from the back of her neck, continuing his seductive explorations.

"Please, Nick. We—we need to face this honestly." She edged away from him.

Nicked sighed. "Making love just now has been the most honest thing between us since we began again."

"But we haven't begun again. Not in the same way as before. Last time I thought we were heading for something permanent. I was expecting a future. The only future I see now is the one I am making for myself. After Wimbledon I'm going to New York, starting my new job, and—and I'm going to work my hardest at putting aside . . ."

"How about another compromise?" he said, his eyes sparkling with humor. He didn't believe one word she was saying. Annie couldn't push her feelings for him aside any more than he could cast aside his own. She was still trying to play it safe.

"What kind of compromise?" she asked warily. She knew he didn't believe her. Nick was so sure he knew her, but Annie had come to many realizations these past ten months. She understood that loving someone doesn't protect you from pain and it doesn't negate accepting what's best for you. Annie's body could still respond to Nick, as could her heart. But her mind was in a place she felt he couldn't reach. And as much as her body told her she could not resist Nick physically, emotionally she was determined to accept this time with him as nothing more than an interlude.

"You've got that look in your eye that tells me you aren't really going to listen to my suggestion," Nick teased.

"I'm listening," Annie insisted.

"Okay. I think we should treat this in the same way we're treating my ankle. Suspend judgment until the time for decisions arrives. Until then"—he paused for a second to gaze down her body with those darkly sensual eyes of his— "let's take each moment as it comes."

Annie sighed. "I don't know, Nick. If I start compromising too much, I might get more compromised than is best for me." She ignored his laugh. "And another thing. I am not thrilled, to say the least, at the thought of our—our lives being broadcast and printed around the world. I do not care to pick up a newspaper to read the latest gossip about your current exploits—even if they are with me. Especially if they are, in fact. I'm most definitely not interested in selling tickets," she concluded hotly.

"Well then, beautiful." Nick grinned. "You've

got yourself a problem. How exactly do you plan to keep tongues from wagging as we walk out of this room and go upstairs with one towel between us?"

Annie looked at Nick, then at herself, and lastly at her heap of wet clothes. For a woman determined to preserve her privacy, this situation created quite a predicament. And Nick's laughter was not helping matters.

CHAPTER SEVEN

By some miracle Annie had managed to make it up to her room unseen by any of the tennis group or press. Dressed in Nick's sweat suit, her own clothes in a tight, damp bundle under one arm, she was not the picture of casual elegance. Nick was less conspicuous in his bathing trunks, the white towel nonchalantly draped over one shoulder. Luckily, it was a glorious day and everyone must have been out sunning themselves or exploring the fabulous Swiss countryside.

Annie joined Nick and a group of other tennis players for dinner that evening. She chose a seat beside Barbara Reese and spent the entire meal trying to ignore Nick's inviting smiles. When the whole group went into the lounge afterward to dance, Annie excused herself, begging a headache. Her body was still feeling too vulnerable to risk some cheek-to-cheek fox-trotting with Nick in a public place.

The next morning it was Nick who came knocking on Annie's door, rousing her from sleep.

"Sleeping on the job," he teased.

Annie's mind was still groggy. Squinting, she checked the alarm clock on the desk. It read seven o'clock. She had set it for seven-thirty.

"The job doesn't start till nine," she protested. "I reserved the exercise room from nine to ten."

"And when do we have the Jacuzzi?" He asked with an intentionally lecherous smile.

"Oh, no," she cried. "I'm not sneaking up back stairs again with my clothes leaving a wet trail behind me."

"Who told you to jump into the water fully dressed? I guess you couldn't fight off your lust another moment."

Annie tossed her pillow at him. He leaped out of its path.

"You can move fast enough on that bum leg of yours. Maybe you don't need whirlpools today."

He exaggerated a limp as he walked over to her. As soon as he got close enough he grabbed hold of her and threw her with him onto the bed. "No, Doc. Honest. I'm hurting bad again. I'm sure I need a repeat dose of yesterday's treatment, but if you want to skip the exercises you can treat me right here."

"Let me have a look at that ankle," she demanded, trying at the same time to squirm out of his grasp.

"First check my heart, Doc. I think its gone plum out of whack."

He caught her palm and slid it under his polo shirt. "See what I mean?" he whispered, his other hand reaching into the opening of her light cotton nightgown. "Your heart isn't doing much better."

"And I suppose you know what to do about it?"

"I can give you the diagnosis, the treatment, and even the prognosis." He nuzzled his face into the crook of her neck.

"Well, I think I can guess your diagnosis and treatment, so tell me the prognosis." Annie pulled back far enough to look at him.

"Hmmm. It depends on a great many factors."

"Oh, really." Annie grimaced. "Like what?"

"Like how fully you cooperate with the treatment. If you fight it, I'm afraid you might suffer terrible setbacks. It could get very frustrating, if you follow my drift," he murmured in a throaty voice.

She was following his drift as well as his hands, which were busily lifting up her gown. Annie could feel her nipples growing hard beneath his expert touch. His caresses were playful, light, and provocative.

And they were having exactly the effect he intended.

Annie sank her head onto the pillows after Nick had tugged her nightgown off, tossing it onto the floor. She watched with increasing arousal as Nick easily slipped out of his clothes and curled up next to her on the bed.

Annie's body was still warm from sleep as he pressed her to him with a sigh. This was what he had thought about all last evening, dreamed about all last night. This morning it had been all he could manage not to come knocking at her door at dawn. He had waited so many hours that now he found himself unable to prolong his desire to have her. His urgency surprised him, but not as much as his surprise at Annie's own immediate response.

After they made love, they both enjoyed the luxury of playful caresses, long, lingering kisses, tender glances, and whispered words of approval. They were ready again for more serious pleasure when Annie's alarm brought a shrill halt to everything.

"Time to get up," Annie murmured.

"I am up," he teased.

Annie shot an arched glance down his body and laughed.

"Go turn off the alarm clock," she said, giving him a little push.

"Turning vicious again, are you?" He got up and leaned over her. "I'm going to have to find a treatment for that, too." He grinned and playfully bit her lower lip. Then he walked over to the table and shut off the blaring sound of the alarm.

Annie stretched. Nick watched with appreciation. "You have a deliciously beautiful body," he said, inhaling slowly.

"Appreciate it from afar, or we will never get down to that exercise room." She slipped out of bed and walked over to the bathroom. "You better get dressed and meet me downstairs."

132

He sighed with disappointment. "What's the matter? Don't you trust me?"

"Your treatment plan is going to wear me out before I get into mine." She opened the bathroom door and looked back at Nick, who was reluctantly getting dressed. "And don't let anyone see you slipping out of my room."

"Don't worry. I'll tell whoever is out there that I was suffering badly and needed some emergency treatment from my doctor." He laughed as she shook her head, mumbling that he was impossible and firmly shutting the bathroom door behind her.

The opening match was at seven P.M. By three o'clock Annie was beginning to reconsider her prognosis. Nick's ankle looked good. All of the swelling had gone down; he had been able to go through the exercises with increased ease; and when Annie carefully examined the injured area she detected no tenderness.

"You really do seem to heal fast," she concluded, her tone still a bit skeptical. She would have bet anything that he would not be in shape at this point.

"It's because of your fine skill and your loving care." Nick grinned. "So, do I get my permission slip to play or not?"

"Are you sure you aren't feeling any soreness or weakness?"

"I still feel weak, but it has nothing to do with my ankle. If I didn't need to conserve all my energy for the match tonight, I'd readily give in to that weakness." He planted a moist kiss on her lips and shrugged. "Ah, the things an athlete must suffer."

"Do me a favor. Suffer in silence." Annie grinned. "Since you are going to be busy conserving your energy, I am going to meet Barbara for an afternoon of shopping and sightseeing."

"Don't go off and forget about me," he teased. "You're back on duty at six. I'm lousy at wrapping bandages."

"I'll be there." She placed a tender kiss on his cheek. "You aren't an easy man to forget," she whispered.

The little town of Gstaad was brimming with summer tourists. The shopkeepers in their quaint little shops were busily selling lace by the yard, famous Swiss watches and knives, chocolates of every possible variety, picture postcards of the monumental, breathtaking Alps, and myriads of other souvenirs. The town itself looked much like a picture postcard.

"Protect me, Barbara," Annie entreated. "I'm a complete pushover for every trinket in this town." She had already picked up a number of them to send to friends and family back home, as well as a few personal souvenirs she was unable to resist. She had also purchased a very large beach towel with the village of Gstaad displayed on one side. She planned to give that one to Nick, so she could borrow it next time she needed a cover.

"Come on." Barbara grabbed her elbow, steering her toward a little outdoor café. "I'm tired just watching you load up with all that junk. Besides, I'm hungry."

"Of course you are. You're eating for two now," Annie said with a grin.

Barbara frowned.

"You still haven't told him," Annie scolded lightly. "Barbara . . ."

"No speeches, please. I've given myself the full gamut of arguments. I just can't seem to get myself to listen."

They found an empty table in the shade. Annie stuck her bundles on the floor and accepted the menu from a tall, good-looking waiter. Swiss men all seemed ruggedly attractive and robustly healthy. It must be the mountain air, Annie decided, sure that the man waiting on them had no doubt climbed the Matterhorn and spent all winter skiing every slope in Switzerland.

"Quite a hunk," Barbara teased, watching Annie gaze appreciatively at the waiter walking away.

"Careful, you're a married woman." Annie bit her tongue. "Sorry, that was a thoughtless remark."

"Relax, Annie. Looking is no crime. Anyway, I wasn't interested, but I thought you were."

Annie laughed. See, she told herself, you haven't totally lost your senses. If a good-looking guy can catch your eye you can't have completely fallen under Nick's spell.

"Every man under sixty seems to exude sex appeal in this town." Annie laughed, pleased to see that Barbara seemed less uptight. She looked better, too. Annie hoped things would work out for her and Jeff.

"You're footloose and fancy free. Why not find out if their looks are deceiving?" Barbara grinned.

"Hey, slow down. I didn't come here to find a mate, friend. This is strictly a business jaunt."

"Ah, hah." Barbara smirked. "Last night at dinner our friend Nick's glances in your direction did not look very businesslike."

Annie started to protest, but Barbara patted her on the shoulder. "Don't worry. I don't think anyone else noticed."

"Sure." Annie groaned. "We're probably already making headlines all over the hotel." She looked across at Barbara. "I'm struggling with some of the same issues as you are."

"You can't be pregnant—at least, you can't know about it *this* fast."

"No, I'm not talking about that." Annie grimaced. "God, that's all I would need. I'm very careful, thank you." She looked across at the mountains surrounding the town for a minute and then looked back at Barbara.

"I have so many doubts. Nick has a way of getting under my skin." Annie's cheeks reddened. "I don't want anybody to know about me and Nick because people are going to make it into something it isn't. Whatever goes on between us is only going to last for the duration of this trip."

"Is that what Nick wants, too?" Barbara asked softly.

"I am never really sure what Nick wants—except to win. But I know what I want. I want a regular, everyday kind of guy who is happy going off to the office each day and coming home to his pipe and slippers. I don't want a superstar. Especially not one who loves every damn moment of it, regardless of the price he has to pay."

Barbara nodded, fully understanding Annie's feelings. She had frequently felt them herself. But she also knew that loving someone deeply enough makes you tell yourself you can cope. Or at least go down trying. Right now she was on shaky enough ground to keep her philosophy to herself.

"Let's order giant ice-cream sundaes with some of that fabulous Tobler chocolate sauce and skip the main meal." Annie smiled. "I love to drown my depression in dessert."

"Be my guest. But me and my little one need some good old protein and iron."

When the waiter came by for the order Barbara chose baby beef liver smothered in onions and topped with the perennial fried egg. Annie ordered chocolate ice cream with hot fudge and told the waiter not to spare the calories. He gave her an admiring smile, the message clear that he thought she could afford all those calories.

* * *

There was an undercurrent of tension in the locker rooms that night. After Annie had bandaged Nick's ankle, first satisfying herself that he really was okay, she joined Mac in the stands to watch the games. Nick was playing a fellow from England who was new to the circuit and far from a top-seeded player. Nick would hopefully be able to take him easily, with no undo stress to his leg.

"Why is everybody so tense?" Annie asked Mac before the match started. She was aware that the start of a tournament was always a tense time, but there seemed to me more strain than she ever remembered from her touring days.

"That damn Council is doing a number on each one of them."

This was the first Annie had heard of the investigation, and after Mac filled her in on the past goings-on he told her the Council was meeting this week and next and would be calling several of the players before the board. Suspensions and fines were on everybody's mind. Nobody knew who was going to get called on the carpet, so it left nothing but rumor and suppositions.

"No one is lily white in any pro sport. But I don't personally know one tennis player who has been into anything really dirty," Mac said, grunting. "Bribes, payoff money, hard drugs—that just isn't the scene I know. Maybe I'm getting old and senile and this stuff is going on without my being able to spot it." He quickly added, "But I doubt it."

"If there is nothing going on, then the Council won't have much of a case against anyone."

"Don't be naive, Annie. You can always dig up some dirt if you look long enough and hard enough. I'm sure the Council doesn't want to go around looking like a bunch of fools. They can make a federal case out of the smallest infraction of the rules to justify all their time and effort."

Mac's words hit a particularly sore spot for Annie. Ten months ago Nick had accused her of doing much the same thing as Mac was now accusing the tennis council of doing: making mountains out of molehills. She hadn't agreed with Nick and she found herself questioning Mac's beliefs. The council might have more of the facts at their fingertips than Mac could know about. She started hoping those facts did not involve Nick. If he were to get suspended for some action now, it would be emotionally devastating. He was putting everything he had into this season.

Annie tried not to think about the whole thing as she watched Nick play. She still had an eagle eye out for any signs of distress on Nick's face, but he seemed to be having as easy a time of it as she had guessed he would.

She greeted him in the locker room after his win.

"How shall we celebrate?" he asked when Mac and the others had cleared out.

"Barbara and Jeff invited us along for a late dinner," Annie said, smiling. If Barbara continued to eat as heartily for two as she was doing now, Jeff wouldn't have to be told anything.

"That's a sadistic smile," he teased, misreading the message. "You just want to make sure we're not alone. And I had such great ideas for celebrating my win."

"I told Barbara we would love to join them, and I told you we were going to keep a low profile. So can the sexy leers across the table tonight," she warned.

"How about if I stick to undercover operations? No one will spot what my hands might do under the table." Nick backed her up against the wall.

"Somebody may walk in," Annie pleaded as he pressed against her.

"I am going to have my way with you, woman, on this very spot and in full view of any jock or coach who happens by, unless you promise to go off with me tomorrow for the whole day. Just the two of us. I'll sneak out my bedroom window and meet you in some hidden rendezvous if you like, but it's tomorrow or right now." He clasped her breasts for emphasis. "I mean business," he murmured, his hot breath against her ear.

"Tomorrow," Annie said breathlessly. "I promise." She tugged at his hands. "Let me go, Nick."

"You don't sound full of conviction. Are you sure we shouldn't capture the moment?" he teased, letting his fingers glide seductively down the center of her chest.

"I'm sure. I'm sure." Her voice revealed no

added conviction, but Nick laughed and released his hold.

"Let's go find Jeff and Barbara. And now that you've given me tomorrow, I promise to keep my hands in my own lap all through dinner."

"You're so considerate." Annie grinned as she smoothed out the wrinkles on the front of her dress.

"Haven't we passed that church before? Like fifteen minutes ago?" Annie swept some strands of hair from her face as Nick's rented sportscar cruised the narrow village road.

"I think we're lost." Nick shrugged. "We'll have to spend the rest of our days wandering the little mountain towns; ski our winters away; sun ourselves on the warm slopes all summer . . ."

"Switzerland has made you positively poetic." Annie laughed. "But you still have a rotten sense of direction. Pull over and I'll check the road map."

"No way. Where's your spirit of adventure? Let's follow this road to wherever it leads." He began singing a Wagnerian aria in his deep baritone.

"You're pretty casual, Mr. Winters. However, by tomorrow I'd place a large wager you'll be making a fast beeline back to Gstaad. Or have you decided not to bother with the finals?"

This was Nick and Annie's third excursion into the Swiss countryside. Every time Nick had a break between matches, he and Annie jumped into his car and raced out to the mountainous hills. They had both begun to relish this time away from the tournament. It was a chance to leave the tensions and infighting behind, especially as a few players had already been served fines and short suspensions from the Pro Council and the general mood was anything but good. More important, Annie and Nick had the opportunity to be alone and get to know each other again.

"Would you look at that!" Nick pointed off to the left. In a fairy-tale setting, rising over the lake of Thun, was a magnificent old castle.

"Let's get a closer look," Annie said, removing her large sunglasses. "It's a beauty."

The Castle of Oberhofen itself was closed to the public for repairs, but the grounds were open. Nick pulled out the picnic basket from the trunk of the car and they dined along the edge of the water, the castle as a backdrop, scattered lakeside chalets shimmering off in the distance.

"What a spot." Annie sighed as she stretched out on the blanket. "I love Switzerland. I think it's the vast contrasts—rugged dangerous mountain peaks in one direction and peaceful, idyllic towns nestled in the gentle rolling hillside; treacherous avalanches and calm, glittering lakes splashed around the countryside like jewels."

"You've become pretty poetic yourself, Doc." He stretched out beside her. "It has been great, hasn't it, Annie?"

She put her arms around his neck and kissed

him lightly on the lips. "Mmmm. Great." She smiled, skimming her fingers across his mustache. "I don't think I've ever seen you more relaxed and—and happy, Nick. The countryside has done wonders for you."

"You've done wonders for me, Annie."

She began to look away but Nick held her fast, his eyes the color of dark velvet. "I'm in love with you, Annie. I don't want things to end with this tour."

"Nick, I . . ."

"I love you," he repeated, capturing her shoulders and drawing her to him. "Listen to me for a minute before you say anything," he told her, punctuating his words with a deep kiss. He lifted her head so that their eyes would meet again.

"I've never seen you happier or more relaxed, either. We could go on like this for a long while. I feel whole again, Annie—physically and emotionally. And I owe that to you. Extend your commitment—maybe take on a position as tour physician if I'm not enough of a challenge." He grinned.

Annie shook her head. "Nick, I can't do that." She reached up and took his hands from her face and held them in her lap. "This has been a beautiful, magical interlude. But it isn't real life. Not the kind I want for a lifetime."

"What's wrong with enjoying life?" he said, his tone cooler. "Is self-sacrifice all that matters to you; slaving away at some drab, dingy hospital . . ."

"It isn't self-sacrifice. Although maybe if you had a little of that quality, it would help you understand what I care about. There are kids out there, kids who might never have a chance to—to do what you're doing right now. They'll never be athletes—some of them might never even walk right." She took a deep breath. "Oh, Nick, let's not ruin this time together. I don't want to fight. Or go over again for the hundredth time that we see the world through different eyes."

Annie was surprised at Nick's silence. She had expected his usual counterattack. But the look in his eyes did not reflect anger—only hurt. She traced the outline of his jaw. "Nick, I'm sorry. I—"

"No, don't apologize, Annie. I let myself think for a minute there that you had changed. It wasn't fair of me. You made it clear right from the start that this was a temporary assignment. And I know you are doing this out of caring and compassion. I can't very well tear you down for just the qualities that make me love you." He picked up a bottle of wine and poured them each a drink. Lifting his glass to hers, he said in a low, sad voice, "Here's to our idyllic interlude."

Nick was off the day before the semifinals, but he was in no mood for a ride in the country. After their last outing he and Annie had pulled back a little. It was not a deliberate maneuver so much as a need to protect themselves. Things had been moving too fast and they each felt it was time to slow down the pace.

There was a message in his box at the hotel. While he stood at the desk opening it, Jeff came by. He looked awful.

"I see you got one, too." Jeff's voice rang with resentment. "A formal invitation to appear before the firing squad. Nice of them to ask us, don't you think?"

Nick read the note silently. It confirmed Jeff's statement. "What the . . ."

"I know how you feel, buddy. They've got great timing—right before our doubles final."

"They can't have anything against me," Nick muttered more in amazement than outrage.

Annie stepped out of the elevator and walked over to the two men.

"Well, we'll just see about this," Nick growled, and stomped off without so much as a nod to Annie.

"What was that all about?" Annie asked Jeff.

"Nick and I are going to be shot at sunset. I'd better go tell Barbara. She'll probably want to dress up for the occasion," he said sarcastically. He and Barbara had been arguing all week. This morning she had threatened to go home before his big match. And now this.

Annie was shaken. She couldn't believe the Council was bringing Nick up on charges. She went looking for him. His car wasn't in the parking lot. One of the tennis players told her he had seen Nick peel out of the place and head for the mountains.

She kept checking her watch, going outside every now and then to see if she could spot Nick's car back in the lot. After a few hours of worry she gave way to her anger. Nick hadn't turned to her; hadn't wanted to share his worry with her. He had excluded her. Annie did not like feeling shut out. She tried to rationalize his behavior. He was impulsive, hotheaded, stubborn; he probably didn't want to burden her with new problems; everyone needed time alone. She still felt angry—and hurt.

Nick and Jeff had back to back appointments with the board in the late afternoon. Annie kept telling herself to stay away, but at the last minute she walked over to the building where the meetings were being held.

Nick was just coming out the door. Annie hesitated and then went toward him. Nick's eyes revealed cold rage. When he saw Annie, he gave her a twisted smile.

"What happened Nick?" Annie's voice was soft.

"Hey, don't look so worried. They didn't want to shoot me after all. They only wanted me to hold the gun to shoot Jeff."

He started walking rapidly, Annie having to run to keep up with him. She finally was able to pull him to a halt.

"Will you please stand still for a minute and tell me exactly what is going on," Annie said angrily.

Her anger seemed to make Nick stop seeth-

146

ing. He looked at her, the expression in his dark eyes switching to bewilderment.

"They wanted me to testify against Jeff. They think he's been taking money under the table for a large number of tournaments. They asked me what I knew about it."

"What did you tell them?"

"I told them the truth. I don't know a thing. I also told them I was sure Jeff wouldn't get caught up in those kinds of games."

"What happens now?"

"They are going to make their decision tomorrow at ten in the morning. It could mean a suspension for Jeff. They sure know how to time things, those guys. It will make big news if Jeff is suspended right before our finals match. They're out to set an example and they've chosen Jeff as their biggest scapegoat."

"Then you won't be able to play tomorrow if Jeff is thrown out."

"You've got it, sweetheart. They might as well jab me in the gut a little, too. Keep me and all the other players in line." That seething look came back in his eyes and he was about to go bounding off again.

"Is that what you're really worried about, that you won't be able to play tomorrow?" Her words were curt and biting. They stopped Nick in his tracks.

"Jeff happens to be my friend. And despite your obviously low opinion of me I am a hell of a lot more concerned about him and what this is going to do to his career than I am about playing a damn match tomorrow." His mouth tightened into a harsh line.

"I'm sorry, Nick. That was a rotten thing for me to say."

They stood only a few feet apart, but Annie was conscious of a gap deeper than she'd felt in a long time. Nick held his pose like an implacable statue.

And then he bridged the gap. He moved toward her and put his arms around her. Annie molded herself against him, her hands reaching round to his neck. She pressed her cheek against his shoulder. They held on to each other for a long moment, then walked together, Nick's arm around Annie, hers slung around his waist.

Their steps took them to the center court, empty now after a full day of games. The maintenance crew was busily readying the area for tomorrow's matches. Nick and Annie climbed up to the stands and sat down. Annie slipped her hand in Nick's.

"I care about Jeff, too. And Barbara. As if they didn't have enough problems. Why would the Council pick on him?" Annie asked with frustration. She expected Nick to come quickly to Jeff's defense. Instead he shook his head sadly, his brow deeply furrowed.

"Jeff's like a brother to me. I'd stand by him in a burning ship. We've been through a lot together." He looked over at Annie, a splitting headache pounding away at his temples. "The worst part of it is—I think he may be guilty."

"Nick . . ."

148

"That's what is tearing at my gut. Jeff has always gone through money like water. He spends it as fast as he makes it and . . . oh God, I don't know. Even if he is guilty, they don't have to destroy the man."

"Maybe they won't suspend him. Maybe they'll only throw a big fine at Jeff."

"I doubt it." He put his arm around Annie, gently guiding her head to his shoulder. "We'll have to wait for the verdict tomorrow."

After her feelings of being abandoned all day, Annie felt a bittersweet sense of contentment as she nestled against him. She and Nick had found each other once again.

CHAPTER EIGHT

"I'm sorry, Mr. Winters, but our decision has been made. This is no longer your concern." Cal Prescott was getting quite heated around the collar. His voice, though low and steady, held a note of growing agitation. He reached into his pocket for his pipe and thumped it against his palm.

"The hell it doesn't. I'd like to see the evidence you have against Reese. I want to know where you esteemed gentlemen come off giving him a two-month suspension." Nick swept his seering gaze across the table at every one of the five men who made up the Council.

A small, nervous fellow at the end spoke. "We are not required to show our records to you, Winters. Anyway, shouldn't Jeff Reese fight his own battles?"

"Calm down, Don." Again Prescott took charge. "We would all do well to take it easy. Now, look, Winters, we understand your concern—as well as the unfortunate position it puts you in. I know it must seem unfair to you to have to step out of the doubles match because of

Reese's behavior. But look at it from our point of view. . . ."

"No," Nick said hotly, "you look at it from mine. I don't like witch hunts."

"That's uncalled for," Prescott retorted. "You —"

"And," Nick continued, ignoring the head of the Council, "I don't like my friend being made a scapegoat. Do you have any idea what this is going to do to his career, to his self-confidence and self-respect? Okay, okay. Maybe the guy took a little extra money under the table a few times. I'm not even going to argue about it. If he broke the rules a couple of times, slap his hand— hit him in his pocketbook. But don't throw him out for two months. Don't you see what this is going to do to him?"

Cal Prescott stood up. He gathered the folders together and tucked them under his arm. "I'm afraid Jeff Reese should have thought about the consequences of his behavior before he made the decisions he made. Unfortunately, he made those decisions a great many times. Too many for a slap on the hand." He smiled sympathetically. "I hope, Winters, if I ever need someone to back me, I'll have as good a friend as Reese has in you."

Nick watched the five men file out of the room. He felt exhausted and defeated. Even his anger seemed to have exploded into nothingness.

Annie was waiting for him outside on the

front steps. His expression told her all she needed to know. She slipped her hand in his.

"We better go find Jeff," she said after he'd told her what had happened inside. "Before I came to meet you I found a note from Barbara in my mailbox. She and Jeff had a big blowup last night and she took a plane home early this morning."

"Great," he snapped. "Hit a man when he's down. She's got great timing."

Annie was about to come to Barbara's defense but she stopped herself. Nick didn't know all that had been going on between Jeff and Barbara, and Annie had no right to inform him. Besides, Nick was in too bad a temper to be reasoned with.

They looked all over the tennis grounds for Jeff. His car was around so he couldn't have gone far. Neither Nick or Annie said much, but both of them felt a silent fear mounting. A person could withstand just so much. Jeff had been hit from all sides. His career and his marriage were coming unglued. Annie found herself praying, as they stepped up their search, that Jeff wouldn't do anything foolish. Nick was doing quite a bit of praying himself.

When they finally spotted Jeff sitting alone on a park bench a few blocks from the club, Nick and Annie breathed simultaneous sighs of relief. They glanced at each other with knowing smiles and then hurried over to Jeff.

"Hi, friends," Jeff greeted them nonchalantly.

"Is that all you can say?" Nick said sharply.

"I've been worried sick about you," he admitted.

"Me, too," Annie added, sitting beside him. "Barbara left me a note saying she'd gone home."

"What are you going to do?" Nick asked, sitting on the other side of Jeff.

"I'm quitting," he said matter-of-factly.

"You're what?" Nick exploded. "Jeff, that's crazy. It's only two months, man. Next season this will all be swept away with the wash. Don't let those bums—"

"Hold it, Nick." Jeff looked his friend in the eye and took a deep breath. "The Council was right. I've been playing on the edge for a long time. I've been trying to justify my actions the whole while. I'm finished."

"You aren't finished," Nick insisted. "I don't care what you've done. Come on, Jeff, you can get your act together. Hey, so you cut down on some of the big spending, keep your nose clean. You can do it."

Jeff looked from Nick to Annie. "Barbara told me about the baby last night. I'm about to become a father and I'm about to lose my wife at the same time. She wants a separation."

Annie reached her hand out to Jeff's. "Barbara loves you, Jeff. I don't think she really wants a separation."

This was the first Nick had heard of the baby. In his eyes that added even more weight to his argument.

"If there's a kid coming along, all the more reason not to burn your bridges behind you."

"I've been burning my bridges for years—the ones that count the most. I was so caught up in the big money, the glamor, a world that was light-years away from the one I grew up in, that I closed my eyes to everything that had real value. It's taken this suspension and my wife walking out on me carrying my child to make me face some brutal facts." Jeff shook his head grimly. "I only hope it isn't too late."

"What will you do for work?" Nick asked. Tennis had been Jeff's whole life just as it had been Nick's. He couldn't imagine his friend behind a desk in some office pushing papers around.

"Right now I'm going home to beg Barbara to give me a chance to give her and our child the kind of life they deserve. And the kind of life I'm finally coming to see I really want for myself, too. I'm getting old, buddy. I've been hitting the road for a lot of years and it's time to settle down. Maybe you ought to think about that yourself."

"What is that supposed to mean?"

"You ain't getting any younger." He grinned. "Maybe you should quit and give those broken bones of yours a rest."

"No way," Nick charged. "No one is going to push me out of a career I've sweated blood for. I still think you're a fool to let the Council or Barbara manipulate you into giving up something that you've put all of your life into. Well,

I'll tell you something, pal. Nobody manipulates Nick Winters." He stood up and walked off before either Jeff or Annie could say a word.

"He'll calm down. I shouldn't have started preaching to him," Jeff said contritely. He could see Annie was boiling mad. Nick's message had hit her right between the eyes.

"Nick may think you're a fool, but I think you've got courage and—and . . ." The tears came so suddenly they took both her and Jeff by surprise.

"Annie, don't take Nick to heart. He's upset, that's all. And scared."

Annie looked up, puzzled.

"Uh huh, scared," Jeff repeated. "Believe me, I understand. I'm scared, too. Where does a guy go who's been involved in one profession since he was hardly more than a kid? It's all we both know and it's been our whole life for a long, long time."

"You're willing to face your fears," Annie protested.

"Hey, it took the Rock of Gibraltar crumbling with me clinging to a falling stone to see the light." He smiled.

Annie sighed. "Nick never clings—to anyone or anything—except tennis. I suppose he's lucky his life is so uncomplicated." She smiled slightly and walked away.

Annie could feel her throat keep tightening up as she walked. She kept her eyes down, watching her own footsteps as she followed the path through the park. Every now and then she sidestepped a bicyclist or a mother with her child in tow. Her path led to a small pond ringed by wooden benches.

She sat down and studied a group of children busy with their sailboats at the edge of the water. She watched the sturdy little vessels set out to sea; listened to the delighted squeals of the small captains; and wondered for the first time in a long while what it would be like to have a child of her own.

Was that part of why she had decided to work with children? Was she trying to create in her career something she believed would never happen in her personal life? She shook her head imperceptibly from side to side. Why couldn't she have it? she argued. I'm an attractive, successful woman with plenty of childbearing years ahead of me. All I need is to find the right guy, get hitched, and then proceed to juggle home and career like thousands of other fulfilled women. She smiled. How many articles had actually been published, she wondered, about the new successful woman who had learned how to have her two worlds—home and career—and live joyfully satisfied ever after?

I've got to stop this affair with Nick. The thought flew into her mind and lodged itself there, edging out the other, safer ramblings. Look at Jeff and Barbara. The strain in their relationship had finally reached the breaking point. Whether they could still work things out Annie didn't know. When push turns to shove, love is only one element in a relationship, Annie concluded. There was the old saying, "You can't live on love alone," and she realized for the first time how true it was. Commitment. That was the ingredient that was also needed. And unfortunately that was the essential element missing in her relationship with Nick. Nick's only commitment was to his career. Everything else came second. And Annie could never be satisfied with that position. She wasn't asking to be first. Only to be on equal ground.

When she got back to the hotel she found Nick waiting for her in the lobby.

"How's Jeff?" Nick assumed Annie had spent all this time talking with his friend. Instead, she'd been making some serious decisions about herself and Nick.

"I think he's terrific," she said honestly. "Probably for the first time in ages."

Nick opened his mouth to argue and then changed his mind.

"Do you want to take a drive? I'll get the kitchen to pack us a basket lunch and we can go get lost for a while."

"No, Nick," she answered bluntly. "I'm tired of getting lost." It was time for her to stop fooling herself and Nick. If she was going to stop heading down this one-way street leading nowhere, then she had better slam on her brakes now.

"Annie, I know you're upset about Jeff and Barbara, but don't let your feelings spread over to us. Their problems aren't our problems."

"That's where you're wrong, Nick. I'm sorry I didn't understand that before." She turned away and headed toward the elevator. Nick followed her.

"Please, Nick, I don't want to talk now."

"I do."

She stepped into the elevator and they rode up to her floor in silence. Their footsteps were cushioned by the deep pile carpeting as they walked together down the hall. Annie heard the echo of their steps anyway and it sounded painfully hollow.

At her door she turned. "Nick, it isn't going to work. I—I thought I could juggle my professional and personal life on this trip, but I can't."

"Open the door," he ordered. "You are not going to decide our lives while standing in a hallway."

She sighed and slid her key into the lock. Nick pushed the door open and nudged her inside. He shut the door behind them.

Before Annie had the chance to move more than a couple of feet away from the door Nick grabbed her arm and spun her around. Her protest got lost as his lips descended. His kiss was both breathlessly passionate and ruthless. Annie tried to struggle but Nick had one of her arms pinned behind her back. She was sure he had gone mad. The more she fought the tighter he held her.

And then she wasn't fighting anymore. Nick's aggressive, angry assault softened as Annie began to respond. He released her arm, but she was only half-aware that she moved it around his neck and that his hands were now moving sensuously down the ribbon of her spine. As he lifted her up in his arms and carried her over to the bed he never took his lips from hers. His ruthlessness vanished. He laid her down gently.

She was crying—large, silent teardrops. Nick sat down on the edge of the bed and dropped his head into his hands.

When he looked up Annie's tears had dried. It did not alter the sadness in her eyes; eyes that reflected a depth Nick could not see into.

"You were the one who wanted the interlude," he said in a low voice. "I wanted you. I accepted your terms."

"I shouldn't have made them, Nick. I don't do well with time limits. They start to close in on me."

"Then, don't limit the time. Annie, give us a chance. Don't run away from me because there are problems. You never used to back off from difficulties."

Annie sat up. "I'm not running away. I'm heading toward something. Maybe toward more than even I realized. Sitting alone on a park bench this morning, I thought about how nice it would be to have a child."

"I happen to adore kids," he said as he smiled, eyeing her carefully.

Annie smiled back, but then her eyes grew serious. "I don't want to go through a pregnancy like Barbara's. Let's be honest, Nick. You aren't going to stop playing as long as your ankle holds

159

out. And it has been holding out really well, better than I expected. Even if you have to have surgery at some point, knowing you, you'll probably be out there swinging your racket before the bandages come off. I just don't want to stand there waiting for you to fall apart enough to hang around. That's a hell of a way to get a man. I think I'd better find somebody who wants to make a voluntary commitment."

"I guess my next line should be, I can make that kind of commitment." He stared at her unhappily.

"I never went for lines, remember?" She stared back bleakly, a brave smile on her lips. "I think the time has come to stick to my contract."

Nick stood up and walked slowly to the door. He paused. "I was determined, when we walked in here, to make wild, passionate, intoxicating love with you. I suppose it would have merely been the act of a desperate man." He opened the door.

"See you, Doc."

CHAPTER NINE

There was little indication that Nick was laboring under an injury. The profusion of sweat, the racket throwing, the arguments with the linesmen, were all part of Nick's usual style and expected by the spectators in the Madrid stadium. It was over one hundred degrees in the shade. The heat was doing a number on many of the players, but although Nick's body was drenched in perspiration and his ankle throbbed, he was playing in top form.

Nick's tirades on the court that day cost him two thousand dollars in fines. His tirades had been mounting since Switzerland, as had the fines he'd had to pay for his bad behavior.

His stormy demeanor was as apparent off court as on and it was costing him more than money. He constantly argued with Mac, got into hassles with some of the other players, and a couple of times nearly came to blows with some of the locals at a neighborhood bar. Only with Annie did he keep his cool.

Annie was not as successful with Nick. She may have been able to withdraw from her physical relationship with him, but emotionally she was feeling tied in knots. She was also furious at him. He was pushing himself too hard, putting unnecessary force into his playing, and picking up some of the tournaments he had originally agreed to cancel.

Today, when he walked into the locker room after his match, Annie was waiting for him.

"You don't look too happy," Nick said casually, leaning his racket against the wall. "Aren't you going to congratulate me?"

"What are you trying to do, Nick?" She tried to keep her voice calm. Exploding wasn't going to help either of them.

"Win, of cause." He pursed his lips and shook his head. "I thought you, of all people, understood that." His voice had the same removed, slightly sardonic tone he had been using since that morning in Gstaad three weeks ago.

Annie held out a single sheet of paper.

"I thought you weren't playing Rome." Annie had picked up the month's schedule from Mac that morning. Nick had added several exhibition matches to his schedule. Annie was furious.

"It's so close to Madrid, I figured why not." He sauntered over to the table and sat down. "Aren't you going to tend to my ankle, Doc?"

"I could walk out on you, right now; rip that contract up into little pieces and tell your pals that you are unwilling to follow my medical advice." She walked over to him. "Nick," she said, a note of pleading in her voice, "don't take your

162

feelings out on your body. If you keep this up you aren't going to make it to Wimbledon."

"Drop it, Annie," he warned. "If you want out, then say it. Don't make me into the bad guy so you can go off with a free conscience."

She could feel herself losing her temper. Maybe he was right; maybe she should tell him she wanted out. But she knew if she left now, Nick would play even harder and more carelessly. She might not be as effective as she wished, but she did keep him in good enough shape to play. That was one area where Nick cooperated fully. He never balked at the exercises anymore. In fact he put extra effort and energy into them. It had paid off. His ankle, though tender and sore after a long match, was holding up. He just might be indestructible, she decided.

Without responding to Nick, she reached for his ankle. She did a routine exam.

"It's more swollen than usual. Does that hurt?" She exerted some mild pressure.

Nick winced. "A little," he admitted.

"I think it would be a good idea to take a heat treatment and then stay off it for the rest of the day."

"I had plans for dinner that I was looking forward to. Do I have permission to hobble down to the hotel dining room if I go right back to bed after I eat?"

She ignored the sarcasm and told him that would be fine. She tried to ignore her curiosity about his dinner plans as well.

Annie left the locker room shortly after Nick

sauntered out. She bumped into Mac, who was coming down the hall with a worried look on his face.

"Oh, I'm glad I found you." Mac stopped her. "Listen, I think we better talk about our boy. Things seem to be getting out of hand. Those tantrums of his are beginning to cost big dough. He used to know when enough was enough, but these past few weeks he seems to have forgotten where to draw the line."

"I was on my way back to the hotel for a nice cool shower and some rest. Why don't we meet for dinner and we can talk over some paella?" Annie suggested.

"Good. I'll meet you down in the dining room at seven." Mac waved to someone else down the hall, telling him to wait for him, then quickly tapped Annie on the shoulder and sped off. Annie had been about to tell him that she'd prefer dining at one of the restaurants in town, but he hurried away before she had the chance. She had wanted to avoid meeting Nick and his "plans" at dinner. She could give Mac a call before seven, but in the end her curiosity got the better of her. As long as that was her only feeling she'd be on safe ground. She closed her ears to the warning sounds of the quake underfoot.

That evening she took special pains with her appearance. She chose an eye-catching soft lavender crêpe de chine dress that clung to her tall, slender body like a second skin. She accented her narrow waist with a wide multicolored sash that, with her dark hair and pale coloring, created a striking palette of contrasts.

Mac gave her a low whistle as she walked up to him in the lobby. Heads kept turning in her direction.

"There ought to be a law against looking that good," he said, grinning. "I thought this was a business dinner." He looked down at his slightly crumpled, casual sports jacket and well-worn gray trousers. Mac was not a man who went in big for appearances. "You want me to go doll up?"

Annie laughed. "You look fine. I was just in the mood to put on something new I picked up in town this week."

Mac escorted her into the dining room. Heads continued to turn. Including Nick's. He was sitting a few tables away from where the maître d' sat her and Mac.

Annie smiled casually at the people she knew. When she spotted Nick the smile was not so easy. He was sitting with Stefanie Hayes, one of the particularly attractive players on the circuit. His hand rested lightly on hers across the candlelit table.

Several flashes went off, leaving Nick and his date, then Annie and Mac, blinded. A photographer had snapped photos of both couples in rapid succession and was heading out of the room before they could see clearly.

"Newsmen," Mac growled, ushering Annie to her seat as he rubbed his eyes.

Annie managed to regain her equilibrium.

"What's the matter, Mac? Don't you want to make the gossip columns with me? 'Famous tennis coach Stu MacKenzie dines out with Dr. Annie Kneeland. What's she treating him for?' "

Mac scowled. "They don't have any interest in me. The guys behind the lines never count. Last time I made the gossip or society columns was more years ago than I care to count. And I'm aging faster lately thanks to our boy over there."

Annie did not appreciate Mac's nod in Nick's direction. "Why give Nick more to get riled up over? If he thinks we're sitting here plotting against him, he is not going to be very happy. Let's keep our conversation as private as possible."

"I'm for him, not against him. Only, lately he seems not to realize it. What gives?"

"Why are you asking me?" She gave him a wary look.

"I may be old, honey, but I'm not blind. In Switzerland, Nick was on top of the world. You looked like you were right there with him."

"Mac, you have the wrong idea about Nick and me," Annie protested.

"You trying to tell me that you were simply working medical miracles? And now the treatment has lost its magic?" His shrewd eyes met hers. "I mind my own business in matters of the heart. But when it comes to how Nick plays on the court—that's my territory."

"Why complain? He's playing great. So what if he has some costly tantrums. The man's on a straight winning streak," Annie said insistently.

"You know the signs of collapse better than I do. But I'll offer my opinion anyway. The guy is heading for a grand-slam fall. And I'm scared he's going to land face first before he gets to Wimbledon. If he doesn't pull off Wimbledon this year, then he might as well hang up his racket."

Annie looked away. Mac was saying all the things she already knew. Her eye caught Nick on the dance floor doing a slow two-step with Stefanie. She felt a jab of jealousy. It was followed by a stab of anger. Here she was, conferring with his coach about how to save his career, and there he was, blithely doing his skillful maneuvers on Stefanie. He certainly didn't look like a man in trouble at the moment.

"I'm only his doctor, Mac," Annie said emphatically as she forced her eyes off the dance floor. "I can work at mending his body, but if he insists on increasing his schedule and taking careless risks, that's his problem—and yours. So if you're worried, then talk him out of the insane treadmill he's on."

"That's what I was hoping you could do," Mac said. "When I talk to him it goes in one ear and out the other. Or else he gets so hopping mad that we end up in a screaming match. We always used to be able to fight it out and then sit down and work things out. Lately all we do is the fighting part. I think the guy has really changed." Mac sighed.

There really wasn't anything else to discuss. Mac and Annie ate their dinners, struggled to

167

come up with small talk that neither of them was in the mood for, skipped dessert, and left the dining room. Annie did not look in Nick's direction when she walked out.

When she came down to breakfast the next morning, Nick was sitting at an empty table in the small coffee shop. He was reading the paper, but looked up as the hostess was leading Annie to her table.

"Join me," he said casually.

"All right," Annie answered with an equally nonchalant tone.

He set the paper, a New York edition, on the table.

"Do you mind?" Annie asked, reaching for it.

He placed his hand on the paper. "Don't bother." He smiled. "You take a good picture. Mac doesn't hold up that well under the camera."

"How did you and Stefanie fare?"

"We make a good-looking couple," he commented dryly.

"I'd still like to see for myself," she said, picking up the newspaper and rifling through the pages until she came to the one she was looking for. She glanced at the news photos and read through the column.

"You're helping me sell tickets after all," Nick observed, his lips curved in a wry smile. "An affair may make headlines for a while, but triangles—now, that makes things so much more enticing."

"I'm glad you're pleased," Annie said hotly,

throwing the paper on the table. "If you'll excuse me, I've lost my appetite."

Nick watched her walk out, twisted the newspaper in his direction, and stared down at her picture. She had nearly taken his breath away when she walked into the dining room last night in that lavender dress. She'd looked so beautiful, it literally hurt. When his breakfast arrived he shoved it to the side. He had lost his appetite, too.

Annie carefully lifted the X ray out of the envelope and clipped it up on the screen. She flicked the switch on, illuminating the skeletal structure and stepped a little to the side so that Nick could see it, too.

"I'm warning you; don't shake your head grimly and say a dozen um-hums," Nick joked. Inside he was far from laughing. He had managed to get through the tournaments in Madrid, Rome, and a half-dozen other cities without any major medical problems. Then in yesterday's quarterfinals game in Munich, his luck gave out. He had moved to net for a ground stroke with a lurching motion that forced his bum ankle into a position that it most definitely did not want to be in. He barely made it through the rest of the match. By the time it was over and he had lost, he was in too much pain to care. Mac extricated him from the swarm of reporters and Annie gave them a brief statement indicating that Nick had suffered a minor sprain.

"By the way," Nick continued as Annie studied the negative, "I appreciate what you did yesterday."

Annie looked across at him with a questioning expression. "What was it I did?"

"You gave the reporters just enough to satisfy them without making me out to be a deteriorating cripple on his way out."

Nick's softened gaze unnerved her. She turned abruptly back to the screen. She had almost forgotten that sensual, warm look in his eyes. It had been over ten weeks since she'd seen it. She and Nick had somehow managed to work together all during that time, the hectic schedule and the constant travel keeping them both too occupied to deal with their personal difficulties.

"Your ankle could be worse," she said in her most professional voice. She could still feel Nick's gaze on her. Despite her efforts to remain aloof, inside, her stomach was churning. She missed him. She missed the man she had begun to discover on those country outings in Gstaad. The raw edge between them since those days felt painfully sharp as she stood beside him, feeling his warm breath against her cheek.

"What now?" he asked.

Annie looked sharply at him. Had he read her mind? Could he know the surge of desire that had just shot through her?

Nick was too busy dealing with his own feelings to think about what was going on in Annie's head. He had tried everything these past weeks to rid himself of his frustration and longing for her. Not the constant rounds of tournaments, nor the futile attempts at dating other women, in any way lessened his craving for Annie. Even his anger at her withdrawal did not alleviate his need.

He focused on the dull pain in his ankle, shifting his weight slightly to relieve the pressure. As concerned as he was about his injury, Nick found it easier to concentrate on the pain than on Annie.

She noticed his shift of positions instantly. "Go sit down," she ordered. "We are going to have to put that leg of yours to bed for a couple of days. Then we can resume the exercises and—and hope for the best."

"Well, I'm off for the week anyway," Nick said. Having lost in the quarterfinals meant no further matches in Munich. "You and Mac have got your wish. I'm going to get off the treadmill for a little while, anyway."

Annie grimaced. "A wise choice. Just think, it only took nearly breaking your ankle to bring you to your senses."

"I guess I'm thick skinned. It takes a lot of rough jolts to make me see the light." His look hardened as he spoke.

Annie didn't answer; her blue eyes revealed nothing.

Nick sighed and walked out of the room. Had he turned back around he would have seen her eyes grow moist with a painful longing and lost hope.

* * *

Later that day Annie stopped by Nick's hotel room to see how he was doing. As she had ordered, he was stretched out on his bed. A tray of barely touched food was balanced on the edge of the end table.

"No appetite?"

Nick shrugged.

Annie examined his ankle and bandaged it back up. She handed him some medication, which he took silently. Then he moved his arms behind his head and gazed out the window.

"Shall I get you some magazines or a book?" She offered.

"No."

"Are you just going to lie here for two days in silent depression doing nothing?"

He gave her one of his sarcastic smiles. "I didn't know you dabbled in psychiatry as well as broken bones."

"As a matter of fact, emotions play a big role in getting well physically. And your mood is not going to help your ankle one bit."

Nick caught hold of her arm as she snapped up her medical bag. "So what do you suggest for my emotional state?"

Annie's gaze went from his hand's tight grasp of her wrist to his eyes. There was no mockery in his look.

"How about a truce, Nick?" Her voice was barely above a whisper.

"I want more than a truce."

They were heading into dangerous territory again. Annie's eyes widened, panic washing over her. Nick relinquished his hold. "Okay," he said softly, "a truce."

Annie smiled tentatively. "Good." She picked up her medical bag. "I'll stop by later to see how you are."

"How about dinner in bed?" He grinned. "It would help my appetite, Doc. As well as my emotional state."

Breaking into a wide grin, Annie nodded her consent. "As long as you remember, Nick Winters, that I am not the dessert."

"No," Annie said emphatically. "I can't, Nick."

"Yes, you can. One more."

Nick motioned to the waiter in the open-air beer garden for two more steins.

"Honestly, I'm getting tipsy," Annie laughed.

"I like you tipsy," Nick observed, tipping his chair back. "Your eyes start to sparkle, your cheeks get dappled with a rosy hue, your lips perk up at the edges, and your giggle—your giggle reminds me of when you were a little girl." It also reminded him of other more grown-up times, but Nick was determined to respect their truce. He kept those more sensual memories to himself, not wanting to invite any more nervous looks in Annie's eyes.

After Nick had spent his requisite two days in bed, he was able to get back to regular activities. Now that he and Annie had stopped throwing daggers, they had spent each day exploring Munich together. They were having fun and it felt good to both of them.

Annie giggled again. "I think you're getting a bit tipsy yourself. You're holding an empty mug to your lips."

Nick glanced down at the beer stein and set it down, replacing it with the full one the waiter had just brought over. "I can hold me beer with the rest of them." He laughed, purposely slurring his words. "However, since I have vowed to remove myself from competition this whole week, what do you say we finish these and go for a stroll in the park?"

"I'm ready for that stroll right now. In another minute I might start snoring to the beat of the band."

"You don't snore." The words had come out so naturally Nick didn't stop to think about the images behind them.

"There's always a first time," Annie said, struggling not to let those images engulf her.

Nick stood up and stretched his hand out for her. "Let's walk."

She took his hand and smiled. "Good timing."

They strolled through the Hofgarten, a palace park famous for its exquisite flowerbeds. Every now and then they would stop to admire a particularly outstanding one. Annie favored the more muted arrangements while Nick preferred the bolder, more vibrant splashes of color.

"When I see something so beautiful I wish I were an artist. It must be a fantastic feeling to capture something utterly magnificent onto a canvas." Nick smiled. "Unfortunately, I never made it beyond rudimentary stick figures."

Annie smiled and handed him her tiny Minolta camera. "There's always photography to capture the moment."

Nick took the camera, but instead of focusing it on the flowers he turned to Annie and snapped her picture.

"The moment has been captured." He pressed his palm along her cheek and then handed her back the camera.

Annie could feel her hand tremble as she placed the camera in her purse. Nick had already started walking again.

For a while neither of them spoke. Then Annie asked, "What would you have wanted to do with your life, Nick, if you had turned out as awful in tennis as you were in art?"

She knew he'd heard her question, but he didn't answer for so long she thought he wasn't going to.

"I never thought about any other alternatives. I guess there was always Dad's company, but somehow I never saw myself sitting behind a mammoth corporate desk. My brother, George, loves every minute of it. He's happy being a bigshot vice president; Dad is happy that one of his boys will some day step into his shoes; and I'm happy to keep my tennis sneakers on." He caught Annie's tight smile. "I guess my biggest fear is that if tennis hadn't come along I—I don't know what I would have done with my life. As a kid I never had fantasies about doing anything but playing tennis. I still can't seem to drum up any other fantasies—professionally, that is."

The tightness faded, as did her smile. But a light was dawning. Nick had tried to head her off the track with that last, seductive tag-on, but Annie zeroed in.

"That's it. You're terrified. You think there really are no alternatives," she said more in amazement than in judgment. He always appeared so confident, so capable and strong. All these years Annie had believed Nick loved tennis so much he refused to consider any other career or way of life. The truth hit her like a bolt of lightning. Nick truly believed he could not succeed at anything else. "You're terrified of failing," she said out loud.

"I'm terrified that I couldn't even come up with something to fail at," he corrected her, turning his attention to an open field where a group of children were kicking a soccer ball about. He took Annie's hand. "Come on. Let's go watch the game."

His message was clear. She took his hand and dropped the subject. However, she did not stop thinking about what he had said, and she wasn't sure whether her new understanding of Nick made her feel closer to him or farther apart. It may have explained a lot about his tenacity, but it also presented a bleak prognosis. If Nick could not find another career after tennis that was satisfying and fulfilling, he would become more embittered with time just as she had once pre-dicted.

They sat on the grass, their eyes focused on the soccer game, their minds far off in the distance. The ball suddenly popped over their heads. They both turned to see it land. It fell at the feet of a boy sitting a few yards behind them. The boy stooped awkwardly over to retrieve the ball. His wheelchair almost tipped, but a middle-aged woman sitting close by grabbed one of the handles and steadied the chair while the boy put great effort into throwing the ball back toward the field.

The other children paid little attention to the boy in the wheelchair, pleased only to have the ball back so that they could resume their game. But Nick and Annie both saw the look in the boy's eyes—a wistfully sad yet resolved look that spoke more than words.

When Nick looked back at Annie, whose gaze was still focused on the boy, he saw that her eyes, too, reflected a sadness and a resolve. And something more—a hope. She really cared and she was determined to put her caring into action. He smiled gently at her and took her hand.

"You're a special woman, Annie Kneeland. A very special woman."

They sat holding hands long after the soccer game had ended and long after they had watched the young boy wheel himself down the path and disappear from view.

CHAPTER TEN

"Do you agree with me, Annie?" Mac chewed on his unlit cigar in typical fashion. He had given up smoking them a few months ago, but he had yet to abandon the habit completely.

"Medically, it makes the most sense. Professionally—well, that's between you and Nick." Annie faced Nick frankly. "What are your feelings?"

"I don't know. The French Open is a major event. I hate the idea of missing it." Nick swung his long, well-muscled leg over the arm of the chair. "On the other hand, I'm not going to pretend my ankle hasn't been acting up more lately."

"My thought is, if you skip France and just kind of take it easy for the next few weeks, you will be fit as a fiddle by the opening of Wimbledon." Mac rolled the cigar over in his fingers and plucked it down in an ashtray. "Let's face it, Nick. Wimbledon is the important one. You want to be in the best shape possible when you step into that center court. If you're feeling good, nobody on earth is going to take that cup

away from you—not Gordon, Vostek, or Colliston. You need that cup, buddy. With Wimbledon under your belt you are going to sail into the
U.S. Open on golden wings." He didn't add that
without a win at Wimbledon, his shot at the U.S.
Open would be enormously diminished. Both
physically and psychologically, the loss would
greatly undermine his chances.

Nick knew that anyway and nodded. "Well, if
I'm going to sit out France, then I want to really
put my all into getting in shape for England. Are
you willing to put in overtime, Annie?"

"It isn't going to help to run you ragged, but,
yes, I'll do everything possible to get that ankle
of yours in playing form."

"Here's what we'll do," Mac said, popping the
cigar back into his mouth. "You two go ahead to
England, take in the sights, and take care of the
medical end while I tie up some things in
France, then we'll meet at Wimbledon a week
before the matches start and I'll work your tail
off at practice." He gave Nick a friendly poke in
the gut and grinned. "Have fun, kids."

Annie felt a wave of tension overtake her. She
and Nick had worked hard to keep the truce. It
hadn't been easy. There were times Annie got
so mad at him she literally had to dig her nails
into her palms to keep from exploding. And
then there were the even tougher times when
her sexual longing for him seemed almost un-
bearable. Nick was suffering similar mood
swings and it was amazing that neither one of
them had lost control yet.

Yet. A two-week hiatus alone with Nick in England was the perfect setting for broken truces. Annie was well aware that the scales could tip in either direction—they might have another major blowup or just as easily end up as lovers again. Catching Nick's eye as they sat in the sunlit sitting room of his hotel suite, she saw that Nick understood the dangers, too. But he wasn't looking too worried.

The truth was that Nick had reached the end of his tolerance for truces. He was moving towards a renegotiation, but so far he had kept his moves to himself. Annie might deny it at this point, but she was digging her nails in her palms far less often than she was trying to control her breathing when Nick came too close for comfort. Nick was convinced that two weeks tramping around the romantic English countryside topped off with some wining and dining in London should put Annie in the right frame of mind for reconsidering the terms of their truce.

They boarded the Hovercraft at Calais. The boat resembled a spaceship, its interior reminiscent of an airplane cabin. As they strapped themselves into their seats, Nick took a deep breath. He hoped the Channel was not going to be too choppy. His stomach was not cut out for roller-coaster rides. The Hovercraft was lifted off the water by its gigantic inverse fans and they were off at an amazing clip. As the boat began riding the waves, Nick knew no one had heard his prayers. Never touching the water, the vessel flew over the top of each crest and slid down into the trough. His stomach lurched with each descent of a swell. Roller coasters were tame compared to this endless ride, he decided, clutching the armrest for dear life.

By the time they neared Dover the water had calmed down. Unfortunately, Nick's stomach had not yet gotten the message. As Annie gazed out at the sparkling white cliffs of Dover, Nick observed the other passengers. He saw that many of them looked as green as he felt. Not Annie, though. She was rosy cheeked, bright eyed, and feeling great. She was busy chatting about how breathtaking the cliffs were, while Nick was barely able to breathe at all.

The Hovercraft glided onto shore, floating over the beach. It settled down to rest, neatly placed inside a gigantic white-lined parking space on the black tarmac just in front of the terminal building.

"Any better?" Annie smiled. Nick had insisted all through the voyage over that he was feeling fine, but as his coloring turned the shade of the water they were crossing, his adamancy had waned.

"Shut up," Nick growled. "You have no business looking so cheerful and gorgeous when I'm sinking to the depths—of my stomach."

"I told you to take those seasick pills before we crossed. Remember that cruise to Bermuda last year?"

"Didn't anyone ever teach you not to say, 'I told you so'?" He tugged playfully on her hair

181

and then guided the rented car off the ferry onto the dock. "And speaking of Bermuda—if I remember correctly, you were very good at taking my mind off my stomach."

"Didn't anyone ever teach you it isn't prudent to discuss past affairs?" She kept her eyes on the road as Nick shot her a wide grin.

"No. Not if I'm discussing it with the woman I shared that affair with."

"I'd rather not have the discussion."

"You were the one who brought up Bermuda," Nick reminded her.

"I'm sorry. Let's both put a clamp on reminiscences, okay?" The edge in her voice held more discomfort than irritation.

"Okay," Nick said gently. "They aren't any easier for me, anyway."

They drove to the ancient seacoast town of Rye, an hour's drive from Dover. After their bad start, Nick and Annie sat quietly for most of the ride. It was late afternoon when they turned into the labyrinth of the narrow, cobblestoned streets of the village.

Nick managed to get lost for a good half hour trying to find the Mermaid Inn, a famous old smuggler's hotel immersed in Elizabethan atmosphere. They kept asking people for directions, but every time they set out they invariably ended up back on the main road.

Annie laughed when she spotted the inn as they were about to go by it for the fourth go-around.

"I think your lousy sense of direction is rubbing off on me," she said with a grin.

"Just when I was planning to show you how much better I've gotten." Nick smiled sheepishly. "That was meant to be a backhanded apology."

"I recognized the stroke." She smiled. "You deserve one, too. I'm—I'm a little uptight about all this, Nick."

"I figured that out already." He ruffled her hair and said, "Relax, Annie. Nothing is going to happen that you don't want to happen." His smile was warm enough, but there was a strong challenge in those dark eyes of his.

Oh, great, Annie thought. Now all I have to do is convince myself I honestly don't want anything to happen. She tried hard to keep her expression from exposing any of her feelings as Nick opened the car door for her. If he was going to be on the watch for signs of weakness, Annie was not going to give him one single hint.

Fifteen minutes later they ducked down the low-beamed entry to the old Tudor pub attached to the Mermaid Inn. The pub, like the inn itself, had remained virtually unchanged since the 1400s. The large, dark-wooded room was illuminated by a roaring fireplace and a small glass-paneled door that led to a flowered patio out back.

The total enchantment of the ancient pub was lost on Annie, who was conscious, at that moment, only of her present predicament. As she and Nick sipped pints of bitter in one of the alcoves along the side wall, she stared grimly at the huge stone fireplace that covered one whole side of the room.

"What do we do now?" She looked back at Nick.

"I think we'd better take that last room or we'll end up driving all night. The innkeeper said we were lucky he just got that cancellation. Everything is booked solid in the area because of the music festival."

"I don't want to share a room with you," she said belligerantly. Sticking to her own ground rules was hard enough. She didn't need to throw temptation in her path.

"What's the matter?" He grinned. "Afraid you might not be able to control yourself?"

"You're enjoying this, aren't you?"

"I'm only being practical. This is supposed to be rest and preparation time for me. I don't think driving all night on no sleep is a great way to start out."

"I'm not going to bed with you, Nick. Oh, don't think I haven't spotted your wheels turning. You think I'm weakening; that I'll renege on the truce and we'll have a jolly sexual romp through merry old England."

"I have to admit, the fantasy has crossed my mind." He placed his hand on hers. "Tell me you've had no fantasies." He looked deep in her eyes.

It was the time for truth. "Sure I've had fantasies. You haven't lost your sex appeal, Nick. The problem is, for a while there I lost my mind.

Starting up an affair again is just going to lead to the same place. Wimbledon is only a few weeks away. I want to go back to the States unencumbered. I have to be selfish about the whole thing."

"I don't think you're being selfish. If you were, you'd be giving yourself what you really want," he said pointedly. "But, luv, if you are determined to shield yourself from your true desires," he quipped in his poor imitation of a British accent, "then I say we hit the road, old girl."

"I'll drive and you can sleep," Annie said contritely as they left the inn.

Nick didn't argue. He was feeling petulant and irritated. And he kept having to clear his head of his X-rated visions of Annie nestled beside him on the four-poster bed back at the inn.

A light drizzle was sprinkling the road as they started off. They stopped for dinner in Brighton, a seaside amusement town. In the 1800s Brighton had become a fashionable, elegant resort town. By the turn of the century more glamorous areas were established and Brighton suffered. Recently it had undergone a renaissance. When Annie swung the car by the Royal Pavilion, the exotic, outlandish Indian palace of King George IV, then the Prince of Wales, she was pleased to see that it was in the process of being completely refurbished.

Annie parked on a narrow street behind the palace. Years ago when she'd been in Brighton, she had discovered a quaint little restaurant called the Upper Crust. She wanted to go back now, but she didn't remember where it was exactly. Nick grumbled as she searched for it. The rain was coming down harder as she finally tracked it down. By the time they'd finished dinner, a full-fledged storm was brewing. Nick offered to drive, feeling a little better after an excellent meal of roast beef and Yorkshire pudding, but Annie was adamant that she continue at the wheel. Before they left the restaurant, Nick called ahead for reservations at a hotel he had stayed at in Devonshire last year. The place was popular with tennis players, amateurs and professionals, and it was a good spot to relax for a few days as well as continue with his regimen of exercises.

"I got two single rooms," he told her as they raced to the car through the downpour. "They're not even on the same floor."

"Shut up." She grimaced, trying to get the windshield wipers to speed up. Nick leaned over her and flicked the lever up.

"Thanks," she grumbled. "I know you're sitting there thinking that but for me you'd be cosy and dry in your glorious four-poster bed at the Mermaid." She was thinking the same thing. It didn't help the situation that the car's cloth roof had sprung a leak.

Nick sighed as a large drop of water hit his shoulder and then landed on the door rest. He leaned closer to Annie. "We'll manage, luv." He put his head on her shoulder and closed his eyes.

He awoke abruptly to a sharp nudge in his

cheek. Groggily, he straightened up, his muscles protesting each movement.

Annie was pulled over to the side of a dark, narrow road.

"Don't tell me we're out of gas?" He blinked a few times and checked the petrol meter. Half full.

"We're lost." She looked over at Nick, her blue eyes wide with despair. "I'm tired, I'm wet, I think I'm coming down with a cold, and—I don't have the foggiest idea where the blazes we are. I can't even see out the damn window anymore. I feel like a total fool." She closed her eyes. "Go ahead, tell me what a jerk I am. I behaved like a stupid teen-ager back at that nice, warm, dry inn."

"Come on, sweetheart," Nick whispered in her ear as he drew her to him. "We've weathered worse storms. Shove over to my side and I'll drive for a while."

"Great," Annie said, but she moved over as Nick raced around the car to the driver's seat. "Talk about the blind leading the blind," she said, but managed a smile as Nick squinted through the windshield.

"Never fear, luv. I've been waiting for this moment to redeem myself. You keep those big blue eyes open for any signs."

"Forget it, there hasn't been one sign of life for the last two hours, never mind road signs of any kind."

"Don't be pessimistic," Nick ordered lightly,

and then burst into one of his ear-shattering arias.

He was really into it when Annie screamed for him to stop the car.

"Nick, Nick! Back up. I think I spotted something."

"Are you sure? It is hard enough seeing out the front of this car. It isn't going to be a simple trick to head backward."

"Then pull over."

As soon as he brought the car to a stop along the curb Annie leaped out of the car. A minute later, drenched to the skin but smiling, she hurried back inside.

"Are you crazy, Annie? Look at you. You're soaked to the bone."

"Never mind that. Salvation is near. Or at least I pray it is. A hundred yards back there is a bed-and-breakfast sign. I can't make out the house itself; it's probably down the path. Come on, hurry up. They might have a room for us."

Nick intentionally did not pick up on Annie's use of the singular—room. Desperation has a way of altering people's attitudes. He satisfied himself by grinning silently in the dark.

They could barely make out the cottage until they were nearly on top of it. It was only nine P.M. but there were no lights on. Annie's optimism began to wane. Just then a light appeared in a downstairs window. Then another one. As Nick pulled the car to the front of the house, an outside light flicked on and a woman came rushing outdoors dressed in a knee-length bathrobe, proper rubber macs, and an umbrella.

Twenty minutes later Nick and Annie sat in front of a roaring fire in Mrs. May Newell's drawing room as she poured steaming hot tea for them out of a silver teapot into two bone china cups.

"So fortunate I didn't leave for Chichester to see my sister today. The poor thing has bad rheumatism. But then Clara called and said there was going to be a bad storm and she didn't want to be worrying about me traveling all the way to Chichester. Insisted the pastor's wife would look in on her and that I should stay home. I did so hate to miss the annual flower show tomorrow at the church fête. Last year my entry won honorable mention, can you imagine? I'm no great gardener, of course—but we English all can get a seed started, so to speak."

Mrs. Newell chatted happily as she watched her two young guests savor her special blend of pekoe and black tea—a luxury item she treated herself to each month from the little specialty market over in Shaftesbury.

"I do hope you don't come down with bad colds." She was pleased that they looked so much better after changing out of their soaked clothes. She had insisted on taking the wet items off to the kitchen, where she hung them to dry by her old wood stove.

Annie took another sip of tea. "I feel wonderful now, Mrs. Newell. This is the best cup of tea I think I've ever tasted."

Nick agreed, thanking her once more for taking them in.

"Now, don't go on thanking me again. Taking people into my home is my pleasure as well as my little business. Ever since my husband, Martin, passed on, it's been quite lonely here. We're a rather sleepy little hamlet. Not too much in the way of action, so my two oldest grandchildren complain when they come down from London for a visit. And it's lovely getting acquainted with Americans. Bovington is off the tourist roads, so I see so few people from the United States. I have a cousin who lives in— now, let me see—Baltimore, is it? Yes. That's it. Ever been there?"

"A few times." Nick smiled, trying to stifle a yawn.

"Will you look at me going on and the two of you, poor dears, are exhausted." She ignored Nick and Annie's protests, took the cups from them, set them on the tray along with the teapot, and insisted that they bring it all up to their room to finish. "I have to be at the church early to help them set up for the fête, so you sleep as late as you like and I'll leave you some breakfast to heat up."

Mrs. Newell said good-night, started toward her room downstairs off the kitchen, then hurried back to the hall as Nick and Annie started up the stairs.

"Here's an extra blanket, in case you feel chilled. I'm afraid we don't have central heating like they do in America."

"Thank you for everything, Mrs. Newell," Annie said warmly, taking the blanket from her outstretched hand.

There were two rooms upstairs, but one of them had recently been turned into a nursery for another of Mrs. Newell's grandchildren.

Mrs. Newell had taken it for granted that Nick and Annie were married and had settled them into her one available bedroom, a small but charming room most of which was occupied by a double bed.

As Nick closed the door behind them Annie busily threw the extra blanket over the bed. Then she turned to Nick. "I'm too tired and too relieved to hassle, Nick. So don't give me one of your sheepish grins or any lip. Just get into your side of the bed and go to sleep." She grabbed her nightgown from the case and stomped off to the hall bathroom to get undressed. It was so cold in the house she decided to skip her bath until the morning.

Shivering, she hurried into bed and under the covers. Nick was already settled in. There wasn't a peep coming from his side of the bed.

"Are you asleep?" she whispered.

"Trying."

"Mrs. Newell is a gem, isn't she? Sitting downstairs I felt like I was in the middle of a Dickens novel." She giggled softly. "Let's pop in at the fête before we head on tomorrow."

"Uh hum," he grunted as he turned on his side away from Annie.

"Nick."

"Uhm?"

"Are you still mad we didn't stay at the Mermaid?"

He turned over to face her. "Please go to sleep, Annie. I like to cope with my frustration in peace and quiet."

"You have redeemed yourself," she whispered.

"It's about to be a very short redemption," he sighed.

"Nick, I think I'm about to lose my mind again." She spoke barely above a whisper, but she knew he understood her meaning because they smiled at each other.

"I think you're finally coming to your senses." He slipped his arm around her and pulled her toward him.

"What if Mrs. Newell hears us?" she persisted.

"She'll say, 'Ah, what a happy young couple those two are.'" Nick wiped out her next argument with a kiss.

"I don't think . . ."

"Good. Be quiet, then, and let me make love to you," he sighed, placing a string of kisses down the side of her cheek to her neck.

"Oh, that feels wonderful," Annie murmured as Nick's kisses traveled lower.

His hands were cool against her skin as he undid her nightgown, but Annie's shiver had nothing to do with the temperature. His touch was electric. Her fears and protests died as instinct and longing took over. Arching against him, Annie kissed him hungrily, greedily. She wanted Nick—her body, her spirit cried out for him. His lips claimed hers with a mixture of urgency and tenderness as his hands sought her breast with an almost reverential touch.

Her soft, inviting body received his caresses with an excitement that made her tremble, her breath quickening. Nick captured her eyes with his, wanting them both to see the ecstasy they brought each other. Annie's eyes sparkled with warmth and desire. Her lips silently formed his name as he bent to kiss her again. He moaned softly as her fingertips tantalized him with promises he knew she would keep.

She loved the powerful, taut strength of his body. She loved knowing every inch of him, yet thrilling in the discovery all over again. And she loved the way he kissed her, caressed her, made her feel so utterly alive with burning passion. They were both poised on that thin edge of fulfillment, unable to wait any longer, despite the desire for it all to never end. As he entered her, Annie's eye lids fluttered open for a moment and as he gazed deep inside that blue sea, he saw not only passion but love. Then their eyes closed and they were lost to the dizzying sensations as desire overpowered them. At the peak moment they captured that vital, incomparable fulfillment, and Annie cried out Nick's name with exquisite joy. Whatever happened, he would never forget that moment. They clung to each other afterwards in their sleep, adrift in wonderful fantasies, as reality slipped out the window on that blustery English country night.

* * *

The homemade scones and jam, along with Mrs. Newell's very best tea, were waiting for them when Nick and Annie came downstairs the next morning. They ate the delicacies at the small kitchen table. Today the sky was clear and blessed with that rare British commodity—sunshine. Mrs. Newell had left them a note urging them to take a side trip to the Isle of Wight, which was an island off the coast famous for its good weather and romantic atmosphere. The ferry was only a half hour from Bovington.

"No more boat rides," Nick groaned. "Not when I'm finally feeling on top of the world," he said as he grinned warmly, pulling Annie onto his lap as she chewed on her scone. "See, I knew you would remember how to cure my seasickness. And a few other problems." He took a bite of the scone that she'd brought to her lips, then kissed her.

Annie laughed. "Well, then, what are you worried about? If I know how to remedy the problem, maybe another boat ride is just what the doctor ordered."

An hour later, having stopped briefly at the church fête to say good-bye to Mrs. Newell and praise her lovely flowers, Nick and Annie stood on the top deck of the ferryboat. The Isle of Wight was only a forty-minute trip out to sea and today the water was calm and the ride was easy. When they docked in the famous yachting town of Newport, Nick was still feeling great.

The island was as sunny and romantic as Mrs.

Newell had promised. Ringed by tiny port towns and exquisite sandy beaches, the small isle had been a favorite of Queen Victoria as well as Tennyson and Annie's favorite, Charles Dickens. Wight was probably the only spot in England warm enough for people other than the British actually to swim in the ocean. The southernmost tip of the island, with its rugged cliffs of spectacular multicolored sands, was filled with an almost tropical vegetation.

Nick and Annie followed the signs to Alum Bay, supposedly one of the must-see sights on the island. Neither of them realized they had to ride a T-Bar lift down the steep cliffs in order to get to the famous bay. Nick groaned as Annie chuckled.

"For a tough athlete, Nick Winters, you sure are a chicken."

The bored-looking attendant was unsympathetic to Nick's agitation. He clanked the bar down and ordered him to hold on.

As they rode up and over the peak of the cliff the ocean spread out before them, the mainland perched in the distance. Annie kept urging Nick to turn around in his seat to catch a look at the clay cliffs behind them. They were a spectacular blend of yellows, purples, reds, and greens. Nick could not appreciate the spectacle until his feet touched earth.

Along with the other tourists, Annie bought an empty glass jar from a stand at the beach, and she and Nick collected samples of the colored sands. Nick waited on shore while Annie took a small motor launch out to the Needles, startling chalk monoliths that jutted out of the choppy Channel water like gigantic white blades.

Before they left the island they strolled through Osborne House, Queen Victoria's lavish country estate designed by her beloved Prince Albert. The guides explained that Queen Victoria had insisted the castle stay exactly as she had lived in it, a monument to the memory of the prince she loved. For all its lavish grandeur there was a cosy comfort to the rooms that Victoria and Albert had called home. Annie took dozens of pictures of Nick in the rooms, along the grounds, sitting in the lush gardens. Then Nick photographed her.

"Hey, where's your smile, beautiful?"

"They really loved each other," Annie said pensively, gazing at the castle. "You can actually feel it as you walk through those rooms."

"Dr. Kneeland"—he grinned, coming up to her and planting a kiss on her nose—"I believe behind that medical mind of yours is the heart of a pure romantic."

As Annie smiled, Nick quickly leaned back and snapped her picture. "That's the look I love," he whispered, his lips finding hers in a brief yet tender kiss.

In the early evening, the sun still high on the horizon, Nick pulled into the Manor House Hotel in Moretonhampstead. The superb Jacobian manor house surrounded by hundreds of acres of beautiful Devon countryside was the

196

perfect setting for their romantic mood. Nick and Annie dressed up for dinner, which they ate in the sumptuous dining hall, its ceiling handsomely timbered, the walls paneled in rich old wood. A massive stone fireplace was lit, the blazing logs taking the chill out of the night air.

After dinner they strolled in the gardens, stopped in the lounge for a nightcap, and then went up to their room. Nick had switched their reservation from two singles to one large double.

Nick took Annie in his arms as soon as they stepped inside the door.

"I love you, Annie," he whispered.

"I'd like to bottle this day like we did the sands of Alum Bay," Annie said.

Nick pulled back. "We don't have to do that. We can collect all the rest of our days, not just one."

Annie didn't answer. Instead she came to him, cupped his face with one hand and, with the other, traced the line of his mustache. Then she kissed him, her fingers slipping down to his shirt.

She undressed him slowly, caressing and kissing his warm, firm body. Whenever he began to speak she would silence him with kisses. Tonight was a night for love and Annie refused to let reality into the fantasy that had begun in Mrs. Newell's guest bed that stormy night before.

In three weeks she was going home, and along with the pain that she would carry back, she would at least have these moments of pure bliss to savor and cherish forever. Despite Nick's protests, this was a time to bottle, a bittersweet love affair that would one day soon be a bittersweet memory.

Nick kissed her tears away, knowing what she was thinking and feeling, not wanting to confirm it. It was a night for love and he, too, cast reality and the future to the wind as he drew her to him.

In the morning they woke in each other's arms. Nick tenderly stroked her back as Annie nestled against his chest. Her fingers leisurely skimmed his hard, muscled body and then spread through his disheveled hair. He eased her on top of him. Annie pressed her palms against his shoulders and looked down at him.

"You should start exercising," she teased.

"My plan, exactly." He caught her hands so that she fell hard against him.

The playfulness quickly turned to passion as Nick's caressing hands and lips reawakened a desire that had barely slept in either of them. Their lovemaking was sweet with familiarity. They knew so well what made the other moan with pleasure, tremble with ecstasy, and cry out with longing. Afterward they lay content in each other's arms, neither of them speaking, treasuring the moment and not wanting the spell to be broken.

They ate a light breakfast on the terrace, went for a long walk, and then Annie guided Nick through his strenuous exercise program. In the afternoon they went for a swim and a ride through the moors.

The pattern was the same for three days. And for three nights they loved fully and intensely.

On the fourth afternoon Nick pulled the car into a scenic overlook so that they could take some pictures of the spectacular tors, those rocky pinnacles scattered throughout the wild, foreboding Dartmoor landscape. A field of heather reached out toward the huge rock formations, the soft purple color reminding Nick of the dress Annie had worn in Munich.

A brisk wind whipped around them as they stood gazing at the soaring stones. Nick put his arms around Annie to shelter her. She turned to face him, her hands moving around his shoulders.

"Do you love me, Annie?" he asked suddenly.

"Yes, Nick, I love you." Her smile was open and warm. There was no ambivalence in her voice.

"Marry me, Annie."

"Nick . . ."

"I love you; you love me. We belong together, Annie. It's as simple as that."

"It isn't simple, Nick. It's as complex as—as you are. Here, away from all the pressures and pain of your world, you're one man. You are warm, tender, understanding, funny, and utterly lovable. But when you take that racket in your hand—you're someone else. Someone I don't really know. I can't relate to the man hitting that ball as though his life depended on it. They're both a part of you, Nick. I'd have to accept one with the other. And—I can't. I don't want to spend my life with a defeated man. And I'm not talking about tennis losses."

Driving back to the hotel, she realized she had forgotten to take any photos. The time for capturing moments was gone.

CHAPTER ELEVEN

Annie browsed through the assorted scarves and shawls as Nick sauntered over to the small stand filled with antique maps. Covent Garden, the hectic, bustling hub of what was once London's fruit, vegetable, and flower industry, was doing great business among the summer tourists. The shops selling everything from Gucci bags to frivolous buttons were crammed with customers while window-shoppers filled the huge enclosed area. A wonderful aroma of croissants, spices, and perfumes filtered through the enormous complex.

Annie wasn't in the mood for shopping. For once she did not find the fanciful wares enticing, and as hard as she was trying to spend this week in London in good spirits, her efforts were not terribly successful. Nick offered no help, his mood swinging from sad to sullen.

They had left the southern coast of England shortly after Nick's proposal of marriage. They both felt a need to get away to someplace more frenetic and busy—someplace where their private feelings and thoughts wouldn't continually engulf them. London provided the necessary distraction. They had spent hours at Westminster Abbey; stood on long lines to go on the guided tours of the Tower of London; attempted to cover every floor of the British Museum. They had bought tinned English biscuits from Fortrum and Mason's, woolen scarves from Harrods, and trendy T-shirts from a boutique on Carnaby Street.

For the first few days the sights and constant activity kept them going. By the end of the week the strain began showing through at the seams. There was a particularly bad moment when they passed the Victoria and Albert Museum, memories of their visit to Osborne House on the Isle of Wight causing them both a painful flood of feelings.

"I think we ought to go on to Wimbledon. Mac will be there in a couple of days, and in the meantime, I can start practicing on the courts."

They were sitting at an outdoor table at Tutton's, a festive, overflowing café on the Covent Garden Plaza. A young fellow in a worn Charlie Chaplin outfit was putting on an amusing magic show, in the courtyard in front of the café, for a large crowd of tourists. Annie watched him for a while as she picked at her chef's salad.

"I suppose you're right. We've run out of steam here." She attempted a smile but never quite managed it. "I'm sorry, Nick."

"We've gotten into the habit of saying that to each other. Let's table the apologies. We're both obviously in a hurry to get on with our lives.

You're almost finished with your stint and I'm ready to grab that golden cup at Wimbledon. We both know what we want and we're going after it. So let's wrap up our pleasant little holiday and go back to work."

Annie looked at Nick, his face hard as granite, his dark eyes coolly distant. This, then, would be the image she would carry home with her. She turned away staring blankly at the funny little man in the baggy Chaplin suit.

CAN NICK WINTERS FOLLOW THROUGH TO THE END? The newspaper headline stretched across the sports section of the London *Times*. It was the biggest question on every tennis buff's mind. Nick had torn through the quarterfinals making mincemeat out of his opponents all along the way. And with his wins came protests from the staid British audiences that Nick Winters was turning the stately old game of tennis into a three-ring circus. Nick's ranting and raving was louder and more explosive than ever.

In the quarterfinals against Evan Williams, Nick was almost expelled from the courts. He barely got himself under control to play and win the match.

"What do you want to do? Get thrown out on two legs rather than limp off on one? You get that temper of yours under control, friend, or else pack up and go home, 'cause this is going to be a waste of your time and mine." Mac bit so hard on his cigar that it broke against his teeth.

Disgusted with Nick, he strode out of the locker room.

Nick had never seen Mac so angry, but it had little effect on him. He knew he was behaving disgracefully. Nick was also aware that his self-punishment had been even worse than his insults to the linesmen and referees. His demand for perfection, always a part of him, had taken on an intensity that was overwhelming, as was his blinding need to win this tournament.

Nick was winning matches, but few friends. The British press never had condoned Nick's antics; his bad boy manners were considered boorish by the genteel English. They preferred the games at Wimbledon to be conducted with good old-fashioned reserve. Each year there were articles and columns about Nick's poor behavior. This year the press was more scathing than ever.

"You want to give me hell, too?" Nick looked down at Annie, who was carefully examining his ankle.

"Am I next in line?" she asked wryly.

"Sure. Be my guest."

"Does this hurt?" She pressed her index finger lightly against the swelling.

"Ouch." He grimaced. "No, it feels great."

"This, too." She pressed another spot and watched him wince as he shook his head from side to side.

"Good," she said blithely. "Then, I have nothing to say." Silently she wrapped the bandage on his leg. When she was finished she told him to soak it in a whirlpool for a while.

"Feeling good as you do, you'll probably choose not to bother." She moved toward the door.

Nick grabbed her elbow. He started to say something, then changed his mind, letting her go.

As she opened the door, he said, "I'll take the whirlpool."

"I left you a couple of tablets on the table. Since you're feeling cooperative for the moment, you ought to take them, too."

Annie walked out of the building and crossed the wide tea lawn. It was a sunbaked afternoon, spectator tickets had broken an all-time record, and Annie had to weave through the crowds to get back to the car park. She needed to get away from the manicured lawns, the vibrant green grass courts, and the ever-increasing tensions as the players neared the finals mark. Annie knew Nick would never let up now. There was no point arguing with him, as he had stopped listening to reason the day she'd tried to explain why she couldn't marry him.

Guiding her rented Ford out of the congested parking lot, she had no idea where she was heading. She followed the winding road from the All England Club up Church Road to the thriving center of Wimbledon Village. A small group of children in uniform, gathering in front of a funny-looking gingerbread storefront, caught Annie's attention. Easing the car into a parking spot, she saw that the group was moving inside. The place was called the Polka Street Theater, a children's puppet showplace. Today they were featuring a real Punch and Judy puppet performance. Annie needed a good laugh.

When she stepped into the lobby, she felt a little like Alice in Wonderland passing through the looking glass. Around all the walls were displays of puppets of every size and shape, the craftsmanship ranging from primitive beauty to refined elegance. In the center of the lobby, instead of the traditional candy counter, was a marvelous array of toys, puppets, and colorful decorations set about a make-believe house. A small calliope sat off in the corner, its lilting tune filling the air with a festive note. Down the hall a puppet workshop was busily in progress, children gluing button eyes to woolen sock heads or snipping colorful pieces of string into hair and mustaches.

Annie stood at the door and watched. A little girl came up to her to show off her dragon puppet and then, with natural ease, took Annie's hand and brought her up and down the table to introduce her to all the other puppets.

When the performance began upstairs in the small auditorium everyone cleared the lobby and workshop for the main show. Annie's laughter mingled with those of the others as she watched Judy chasing after Punch, more often than not catching him with her paddle. This was the true art of slapstick and Annie let everything else slip from her mind as she joined in the exuberant fun.

After the show she walked back to her car, waving good-bye to some of the children she had met. She found herself wanting to postpone the ride back to Wimbledon. Those few carefree hours at the theater had revived her, but she knew the tense atmosphere back at the club would be waiting to greet her with open arms.

She was right. As soon as she walked into the clubhouse, she sensed the tightness—restrained and in control but clearly present. It was Happy Hour, only no one looked especially happy. The winners were scared about losing, and the losers were busy counting what they had lost in cash and ranking. Annie saw Mac sitting alone at a small table.

Things were worse than she'd thought. Mac's chewed-up cigar was emitting large billows of smoke. His vow to quit had gone by the wayside —just like everything else.

A white cloud hit her in the face as she sat down across from him.

"I don't think I want to know." She sighed wearily. Whatever had driven Mac back to smoking had to be related to Nick.

"You don't." He inhaled loudly and closed his eyes, letting wifts of smoke slip out of his slightly parted lips.

Annie ordered a gin and tonic and watched Mac as he started to make smoke rings. She wasn't entertained, but, then, he wasn't trying to put on a show.

He leaned forward, moving the cigar out of Annie's direction as she edged away from the stream of smoke.

"You'd better go find him and have a look at his ankle. I told him a couple of hours ago to let up on the practice, so, of course, he goes at it for another hour or more until he ends up limping off the court." He took another deep puff of his cigar, forgetting to keep the fumes out of Annie's face. "Oh yeah, he should do great in the semis tomorrow!"

Annie studied her half-finished drink. If she tracked Nick down now she doubted she'd be tending to his wounds. Not when she felt more like inflicting a few of her own on him. What was the matter with him? He wanted Wimbledon more than anything, but he couldn't be going about the whole thing in a worse manner. It was that damn rage of his. The reins had gotten too loose and he couldn't grab hold of them. Or he didn't want to. Annie shoved her drink to the side of the table. Mac nodded silently as she walked off.

Nick was sitting in the whirlpool giving himself hell. Anger, fear, frustration, whirled around him as swiftly as the pulsating jets. An image of a roller coaster kept flashing through his head. He had bought the ticket, gotten strapped into the seat, and now there was no getting off until the end. In the meantime he had to figure a way to ride it out without crashing. He was making a silent vow to get a better grip on the bar, when Annie walked in.

For an instant the memory of that afternoon in Gstaad swept over them both. Then everything that had happened since that sweet seduction erased the moment.

"Hi, Doc. Checking to see if I follow orders?" Nick asked casually.

"You've driven Mac back to his stinking cigars," Annie retorted. "And you are damn near driving me crazy."

Nick moved to the edge of the whirlpool. "Do you want to hand me my towel or are you liberated enough to stand around fighting with me in my birthday suit?"

She threw the towel to him. He wrapped it around his waist as he stepped out of the water. "Okay, now we can go to round two."

"What are you trying to prove?"

"That I can make it to round three?" He sat down on the edge of a plastic recliner and concentrated on slipping his feet into his rubber thongs.

Annie took the chair next to him. "Nick, I wish I could help. Taking care of that ankle of yours is tough enough, given your determination to test my limits, but you're also testing them in areas I'm not as equipped to cope with."

"You'll be able to stop coping in a few days. In fact, I was thinking that maybe you ought to stop now." He looked over at her for a brief moment, but then returned his gaze to the white-tiled floor.

"No, Nick. If I walk out now you're likely to destroy that ankle of yours. I'm not giving you a chance to blame me for your defeats. My contract ends at your finals match and I intend to see this through to the—"

"To the bitter end?"

"If that's how you want it," Annie said, feeling her anger start to well up.

Nick merely nodded. Annie wasn't sure how to interpret the motion. When he walked out she saw that he wasn't limping. Well, that was one small blessing.

Nick kept reaching out for that bar to steady himself, but the roller coaster seemed to pick up speed as he raced through the semifinals. The day before the finals—that big moment when the two top players swing it out for all they're worth in the world-famous center court at Wimbledon—the sky opened up and a driving rainstorm pelted down.

Nick had worked out all morning, long after Annie had left the exercise room telling him to cool down. There was no cooling down. Nick had to keep moving, the tension driving him on at a fever-pitch speed. Tomorrow he was facing Seth Colliston across the net and Nick didn't try to fool himself into believing he could walk away with the win.

Last year Nick had defeated Colliston in the semifinals at Wimbledon, but last year Colliston was just beginning to break through to the top. This had been a very good twelve months for the young American. He was shrewd, tough, and, like Nick, was embued with that killer instinct that separated the men from the boys out on the court. He had emerged this year as the leading contender for Wimbledon. Nick was going to have to work overtime to pull this win out of the bag.

"What are you still doing down here? I told you to wind up hours ago."

Nick set the barbell down and looked at Annie, whose blue eyes were cool as ice and boring into him.

"I'm not overworking the ankle, Doc, so quit glaring."

"Great. Are you planning to get an elbow or shoulder injury instead?"

"I'm planning to continue my exercises in peace. If anything breaks I'll call for you."

"Will you listen to reason for once in your life? You're setting yourself up for a loss the whole while you tell yourself you have to win. I think that a part of you wants to lose tomorrow. Deep down you already taste that defeat and you—"

"Get off my back," Nick shouted, his face rigid with rage. "I didn't take you on as a psychiatrist, so keep your damn analyses to yourself, do you hear me? Stop worrying about my head, Doc, and stick to my ankle. That's all you're here for. Remember that," he added bitingly.

Annie was trembling with rage. In a voice so tight she couldn't even recognize it, she said, "You don't need me for anything—except maybe to be your private scapegoat. I didn't sign up for that position." She swung around and stormed out of the steamy room, the pelting rain outside no match for her fierce mood.

Colliston had an amazingly wicked serve. And he was feeling great. He had watched Nick Winters for years, studying all of his strengths and weaknesses. The weaknesses were few and far between, but they were there and Seth Colliston had reached a point in his career where he knew how to seek them out. He stepped around the court, intentionally catching Nick's eye, attempting to psych him out with his cool, friendly smile as they changed sides. Nick's scornful gaze reminded Colliston that this was a man who didn't react to those maneuvers. No—Colliston would have to work on the strokes and not the mind.

Nick knew he was facing a man who was determined to be champion. He recognized the look. It was one he'd seen in the mirror endless times. This morning, though, Nick's reflection had been hollow, his brooding features strained and taut. As he gazed in the glass he had found himself looking at a man who had fought long and hard for something only to lose sight of what the fight was really all about. Now he was struggling to stay afloat.

For the first two sets the spectators had no idea Nick was already sinking. Nick blasted Seth Colliston in his inimitable fashion, taking a strong lead in both sets. Colliston's smile was not quite as cool as they changed sides for the third set.

Annie sat quietly in the stands watching. From the moment she'd seen Nick walk into center court this afternoon, she'd known the outcome. If anyone had asked her how she could be so certain, she would not have been able to explain it. He wasn't limping at all, his form and delivery were as exquisite as always, and his shots were right on target every time. When she had walked out on Nick yesterday she'd felt completely justified in her decision to stay off his back as he had ordered. This morning she had called Bill Kenny and told him to see to Nick's ankle. He could bandage it as well as she could, she told herself. And that was all Nick needed.

So why was she feeling so guilty watching him play? He was winning, wasn't he? She'd gotten him to Wimbledon on two feet as promised. She kept trying to convince herself that her blowup with Nick and her staying away this last morning would not affect his game. It certainly didn't seem to be getting in his way.

So why wasn't she the least bit surprised when Colliston took the third set and was handily heading toward a fourth-set win? Pandemonium was breaking loose in the stands as the turnaround took place. Only Annie remained calm. Her worst fears were coming true before her eyes and she felt as helpless as she had yesterday in the face of Nick's rage and pain. She wanted to get away before Nick's ultimate defeat, but something held her riveted. She felt compelled to see it through to the bitter end, after all.

She stayed to watch a beaming Seth Colliston

take the winner's trophy and the hefty sum of money that went along with the victory.

It was the worst defeat Nick had ever suffered. Even last year his loss at Wimbledon had been razor close. Today, Seth Colliston had pummeled the superstar to the ground, humiliating him in front of everyone. Annie felt hot tears sting her cheeks. She wasn't sure whether she was crying because he had lost or because she felt rotten for walking out on him when he needed her most. It was probably a combination of both mingled with her own personal sense of loss.

Annie got herself under control and then hurried to the locker room to find Nick. All she could think about was that she had to be with him. And she was not going to let him browbeat her into storming off again.

Only, Nick wasn't in the locker room. Mac told her he had escaped from a side exit to avoid the press and was probably on his way back to the hotel.

By the time Annie made her way through the crowds, ducking the reporters herself, she ended up in a frustrating traffic jam. It took over forty-five minutes to get to the hotel. Nick had already checked out.

Annie was on her way back to the States. The 747 was once again filled to capacity with summer tourists returning from holiday. They were heading home, back to work.

Annie was going home to work, too. But not until she found Nick and . . .

And what? She didn't think about anything beyond seeing him. She would have to trust her instincts after that.

Mac told Annie that Nick most likely had gone straight on to New Hampshire. He was committed to playing the Volvo Tournament in North Conway and Mac was confident Nick would be there. His pride would get him to the court. According to Mac, Nick would never tolerate the public thinking he was too embarrassed or humiliated by his loss at Wimbledon to show up for a firmly scheduled match. Annie assumed Mac was right.

They were both wrong. Nick didn't show up in North Conway. Mac was getting as worried as Annie. It wasn't like Nick to disappear without a word. Or a trace. No one had heard from Nick since he'd walked off the court at Wimbledon. Mac tried his apartment in New York, his parents' place in Connecticut, and even a couple of old girl friends. He drew a fat zero. Mac filled Annie in on his efforts, save for the calls to the women from Nick's past. Annie had enough on her mind without that information.

They were eating hamburgers in a local North Conway hangout. Mac had managed to give up smoking again, but he was eying his unlit cigar with a wilting resolve. Annie was sympathetic to his struggle. This was a bad week for breaking habits.

"Go on. Light up." Annie smiled.

"That's not very good medical advice," Mac answered wryly.

"I'm speaking as a friend, not a doctor, right now."

Mac picked up the cigar and twirled it around in his hand. Then he resolutely dumped it back in the ashtray.

"No. It's not going to help matters. No sense taking it out on myself." He gave her a no-nonsense look. "No sense you taking it out on yourself, either. And I'm speaking as a friend, not Nick's coach, right now."

Annie's smile broadened. She reached over and squeezed Mac's hand. Then all of a sudden those blue eyes of hers lit up and started sparkling. "Of course," she said.

"Of course?" Mac echoed in a baffled voice.

"Mac, do you have any change? I just realized the person who might have some answers."

Annie made her way through the noisy lunch crowd to the back of the restaurant. Luckily the phone was in a booth or she would never have been able to hear a thing.

After getting the number from information she anxiously dialed, holding her breath as the phone started ringing. This was the best bet she had and if she got nowhere with this call, her worry was going to turn to panic. That was what had triggered off the phone call in the first place. That nagging fear that Nick could do something crazy in his despair reminded her of the day she and Nick had felt that same panic about Jeff Reese.

"Jeff, this is Annie Kneeland."

"Annie, how are you? And where are you?"

"I'm lousy and I'm in New Hampshire looking for Nick."

"You're looking in the wrong place," he said with a chuckle.

"Tell me the right place," she said, feeling a sense of well-being for the first time in weeks. Jeff obviously not only knew where Nick was; he knew Nick was all right.

"Hold on. Barbara wants to speak to you."

"Annie," she heard Barbara say.

"Barbara, what's going on? Where's Nick? Is he okay?"

"Slow down," Barbara said. "Come to New York and visit us. We'll fill you in on all kinds of exciting news."

CHAPTER TWELVE

Barbara Reese put the finishing touches on the chocolate cake.

"No samples," she warned Jeff affectionately as he attempted to dip his index finger into the icing.

She leaned against him as he put his arms around her, his fingers spread over her abdomen.

"Hey, I think junior is waking up. He must smell that cake." He grinned, pressing his lips against her hair.

"He is an active devil. Or she, of course." Barbara placed her own hands by Jeff's. This past month the baby had really begun to kick and Jeff and Barbara agreed it was the most wonderful feeling in the world.

Jeff swung Barbara around. He looked into her warm eyes filled with love, her face radiant with that special glow of impending motherhood, and for the millionth time he thanked his lucky stars that he hadn't lost her. These past few months had been the best of his life. In winning back Barbara he had found himself.

And who knew, maybe he was going to be able to help a good friend find himself, too.

The doorbell rang.

"That must be Annie," Barbara said, smoothing her hair.

"Did I tell you how much I love you and junior, today?" Jeff whispered.

"Go answer the door, you idiot." She laughed, giving him a fast embrace and shoving him to the door while she stepped into the kitchen to make sure everything was set for lunch.

Jeff greeted Annie with his famous bear hug. As Barbara came into the room, Annie quickly checked her reaction, remembering their first meeting in the airport. Today there were no sullen, distrustful glares. Barbara rushed up to Annie, gave her an affectionate squeeze, and led her into the living room.

Annie looked from Barbara to Jeff. The two of them radiated happiness and contentment. For a moment Annie felt a sharp pang of envy, but it did not diminish the joy she felt at seeing the two of them so obviously in love and making a go of it.

"You look tired, Annie," Barbara said as Annie sank into a club chair in the living room.

Annie nodded. "I am, but it's good to see the two of you again. This is a lovely apartment." Annie swept her gaze around the large room painted a soft cocoa color with buttercream trim on the molding. The couch and two matching love-seats grouped around the fireplace were upholstered in a pale blue velour with tiny pinpoint dots of white. The bay window was curtainless, natural wood shutters open to let in the bright sun. On one wall were a half-dozen blow-up photographs of Barbara, all taken during her pregnancy. Annie's eyes rested on them.

"I don't think I've ever seen a more beautiful pregnant woman," Annie said warmly.

"That's because there has never been a happier one!" Barbara laughed, putting her arm around Jeff, who sat beside her.

"It shows—in both of you." Annie's smile faded. "You said you had word about Nick?"

"We have so much to tell you." Barbara smiled. "But first we'll have some lunch, then we'll talk, and then Jeff and I will show you our big surprise."

Annie started to speak, but Jeff interrupted. "Don't argue with her, Annie. The woman has become impossible since she got pregnant. She's practicing for motherhood by insisting on bossing everyone around," he teased. "Anyway, she spent the whole morning making homemade noodles for lunch and, believe me, they are not to be missed."

Annie held back a sigh. Any other time she would have loved a marvelous home-cooked meal with these two people for whom she had come to feel so much affection. But ever since she spoke to them on the phone yesterday, she'd been able to concentrate on only one thing— they knew what was happening with Nick.

Before lunch Barbara showed Annie the new nursery, a bright, cheerful room decorated in bold red, yellow, and green Marimekko wallpaper, a thick grass-green carpet, and shiny new white spindle crib and matching rocker.

"What more could a baby ask for? A room right out of *Beautiful Homes* and two parents filled with loving excitement." Annie hugged Barbara.

Over lunch Jeff and Barbara kept the conversation light. Annie cooperated, given the fact that she had little choice. Her friends were holding all the cards and she trusted them to show her their hands in due time.

As Barbara poured them all steaming cups of cappuccino after lunch, Jeff said, "Remember when Nick asked me what I would do for work if I quit tennis?"

Annie nodded. She remembered that whole encounter verbatim.

"That was one tough question. And I didn't have an answer. I was so worried about patching things up with Barbara that I really didn't think about my career. But after Barbara and I decided we were both going to put everything we had into making this marriage work, well—then I had to figure out some way to pay for my kid's college education." He smiled at his wife. "Nick's told you I used to have quite a free hand with money so when I walked out in Gstaad, let's just say I did not come home to a nice juicy bankroll. Thanks to Barbara, we had something to fall back on. She'd managed to save some money despite my bad spending habits."

"You should see him now, though," Barbara

said with a tender smile. "He's become positively thrifty. Goes shopping and looks for the best bargains, walks around the house shutting off unnecessary lights. He even keeps a budget."

"I need to—now that I've become an administrator."

"An administrator? Nick said he could never imagine you shuffling papers around in some fancy office," Annie remarked.

Barbara and Jeff gave each other knowing grins. "I wouldn't call my place fancy. And most of the time what I'm shuffling doesn't involve papers. I leave most of that stuff to Barbara."

"Okay, you two, you've got my curiosity piqued to the nth degree. Are you going to tell me about this venture of yours or not?"

"Better than that, we'll show you," Barbara said. "The place is a few blocks from here. Let's walk over."

Annie hesitated. So far they hadn't even mentioned Nick. Jeff and Barbara seemed so intent on showing her their new venture that Annie decided to wait until she'd seen it before pursuing her own questions.

Their apartment on East Twenty-third Street in New York City was in a transitional neighborhood where fancy towering apartment and office complexes mingled with groups of old brownstones, like the one the Reeses lived in. A few blocks from their apartment the brownstones appeared less well maintained, the storefronts reflecting the change. Instead of exclusive antique shops, boutiques, and French bakeries, there were record stores, a shoestore with sale shoes sitting on racks out front, a couple of used furniture shops, a small grocery store announcing a host of sale items in bold black letters on the windows, a crowded McDonald's, and across the street an equally packed Burger King.

"I grew up over there," Jeff said, pointing to McDonald's.

"I've heard of growing up backstage, but in a fast-food joint?" Annie laughed.

"As much as I'm not crazy about hamburgers, that place is a big improvement over the apartment house that used to sit on that spot."

"Jeff came back home from Gstaad to find his roots," Barbara explained. "He used to be so busy running away from his past that he forgot the value of knowing who you really are."

"And what you really want," Jeff added.

They walked past an old school building that was all boarded up.

"Your old school?" Annie asked.

"That's it. It's also my new place of business." Jeff announced.

He had that proud papa look again and Annie eyed him with a bewildered smile. "This is it?"

"Actually, it's around back. Two years before they closed the school down, the city built on a new wing that was a combined classroom annex and gymnasium. But then the old part was condemned so the new addition had to go by the wayside. It was sitting here slowly falling apart until I got the city to lease it to me for two years."

As they turned the corner, Annie saw a group of kids standing outside the two-story building. As she came closer she observed, with surprise, that they all had tennis rackets in their hands. She looked over at Jeff and grinned. "Tennis?"

"Tennis is the biggest pitch down here at the Rec Center, but we do a little of every sport. I remembered all those years of playing tennis against the back wall of the school when I was growing up, with all the other kids looking at me like I was nuts, and I thought about the fact that kids from these areas hardly know what a tennis racket looks like and rarely know anything at all about the game or the profession. Why should pro tennis be closed to these kids? Not that I'm trying to turn them into pros. Tennis is a great game and it's about time it moved from the country clubs to the city playgrounds."

"Jeff is doing a fabulous job here. He has really turned some of these kids on to the game and gotten them off the streets and out of trouble. A few of them are very talented, but almost all the kids involved in the program seem to get something out of it. It's nice to watch that skill develop along with self-confidence and a sense of accomplishment." Barbara slipped her hand in Jeff's. Being a part of this program with Jeff had also done wonders for her self-confidence.

"I think it's a terrific idea," Annie said enthusiastically.

"I'm trying for state and federal grants to keep this place going and maybe add on to it. I have some big dreams." Jeff waved and greeted the kids as he opened the door for Annie and Barbara.

"I've also found myself a couple of top people to help me out here," Jeff added as he led the two women down the corridor. The wide hallway was freshly painted in green and white with sports posters and newly scribbled graffiti covering the walls. Stopping in front of his office, Jeff said, "Barbara and I have a couple of things to do in here. Why don't you go down to the gym and watch some lessons and we'll meet you there in a few minutes? The gym is through those large double doors at the end of the hall."

Annie cast a suspicious glance at Jeff and nodded. As she walked toward the swinging doors, she had a pretty good idea that this visit was going to shed some light on her unanswered questions.

When she walked into the gym she spotted Nick immediately. He was busy showing a couple of boys a backstroke. Then he crossed over to the other side of the court and started throwing balls, first to one boy, then the other. Each time either of them swung, Nick shouted out enthusiastic praise.

It really wasn't shock or surprise that Annie experienced finding Nick here. She had realized, walking over to the Center, that Jeff and Barbara were too sensitive to ignore the main reason Annie had rushed to the city. When Jeff had ushered her inside she had a gut feeling Nick might be here. And yet, seeing him in this setting, actually working with these kids and so obviously having a good time, did throw her off.

She stood at the door, moving over to a bench when two young teen-age girls came through. The girls giggled to themselves and went over to the side of the court where Nick was giving his lesson. Nick told the boys to take a break and motioned to the girls to take their places on the court. The boys walked over to a third boy who was sitting on the bench. The three of them watched the lesson and, Annie observed with a smile, the two cute girls in their short shorts and T-shirts. Nick knew the girls by name and chatted with them for a couple of minutes before starting the lesson. Annie kept her eyes on Nick, but he was so involved in teaching he never looked in her direction.

He finally saw her when he went after a wildly placed ball. He stopped in his tracks, his surprised face breaking into a smile, and then a broad grin as he took all of her in. He called back to the girls to take a break and walked over to Annie.

"Hi, Doc."

"Hi."

"How do I look out there?"

"You look—terrific."

"So do you." Nick rested one foot on the bench and leaned closer to her. He put his hands first on her shoulders and then brushed his palm against her smooth-as-silk cheek. "I missed you."

"Hey, Nick, are you going to make time all

afternoon with that chick or are you going to give me my lesson?" The third boy who had been sitting on the bench the whole time Annie had been there had cupped his hands around his mouth, megaphone fashion, and shouted his question across the gym.

Nick turned his head and gave the boy a good-natured grin. "She's a lot prettier than you, Baker, so cool your jets. I'll make you work this afternoon. You better believe it." He turned back to Annie. "Don't run off on me." He grinned devilishly, kissing Annie hard on the lips as she started to give him a large piece of her mind. "I'll be finished in a little while and then you can jab me."

Annie shook her head and grinned. "Hurry up, then. Your students await you, teach."

Barbara and Jeff came into the gym. Jeff walked over to the other court and started giving a lesson to a small group of beginners. Annie caught the knowing look between him and Nick. Barbara joined Annie at the bench.

"Nick's a great instructor. The kids adore him. He's practically slept here all week, teaching a dozen classes, helping Jeff with some of his proposals for grants, even painting a few of the old classrooms. The guy has boundless drive."

"I know," Annie said. "But I never thought he would use it in this way."

"I think Nick has been finding some roots, too." Barbara smiled.

"Here? This place is about as far removed from Nick's roots as anyone could get."

"I'm not talking about environment. I'm talking about what's inside his soul. You only have to watch him out there with those kids to know he's found a part of himself that's been locked away all along."

"I see what you're saying." Annie stared out at Nick. "You have no idea how terrific it would be if he could really see beyond being a superstar with nothing more to look forward to than a life as a retired celebrity."

"Oh, I think I have an idea. Nobody wants to live with a person who feels empty and unfulfilled, whiling away the hours dreaming about past glories and the good old days. I was always scared that Jeff would do that after he finally got too old to play. And now, look at him. I bet if you asked Jeff which were his happiest times he'd tell you: 'Right this minute.' "

"I don't have to ask him. It's written all over his face. And yours."

"Would you and Nick like to come back to our place tonight? Nick has the spare room. His apartment has been sublet until next week. He arrived back in the city a little earlier than expected," Barbara commented, brows arched.

Annie gave her friend a wry grin and said, "Thanks for the invitation, Barbara, but I've already checked into a hotel uptown. I arrived earlier than expected myself. A colleague at St. Mead's has already found me an apartment close to the hospital and it will be ready in a couple of days. I'll stay at the hotel until I can move in. I've decided to start my new job early. I'm going to begin on Monday."

"That's only five days from now. I'll help you get settled—after you and Nick have some time to yourselves. It's going to be so nice having you around, Annie."

"For me, too," Annie agreed.

Nick shouted good-bye to the kids over his shoulder as he walked toward Annie.

Stretching out his hand to her, he said, "Come on, Doc. Let's go play hookey." He grinned across at Barbara. "Okay with you, boss?"

"School's out." She grinned back.

Annie was nervous. On the taxi ride up to her hotel, Nick sat close to her, his arm around her, holding her tight to his side. He only spoke a few whispered words about the apple scent of her hair, the warm silkiness of her skin, the sea-blue warmth of her eyes. He made love to her with his voice, with his lips against her cheek. Annie felt awash with desire just listening to him speak. All she could think about in that taxicab was what it would feel like to have Nick really make love with her again.

Then, walking into the hotel lobby, the nervousness took over. She had told herself on the way to New York that when she saw Nick she would know where things stood and she would know what she wanted. Seeing him at the Rec Center she had felt a real glimmer of hope. Maybe Nick, like Jeff, would find something other than tennis that he could believe in and want. But she wasn't sure. And she was scared to trust her instincts, which told her only to grab hold of her man now that she'd found him.

Nick's instincts were giving him a similar message and he was feeling no ambivalence about trusting them. This past week he had faced a lot of things about himself and the jigsaw pieces of his life were beginning to fall into place. When he had escaped from Wimbledon, he knew he was trying to run away from himself. All his life he had feared failure and then there it was—staring him in the face on the most prestigious center court in the whole world. It had happened—his worst nightmare a reality. If anyone had told him that event was ultimately going to be the most valuable of his whole career he would have punched him in the nose. But the person would have been right. He had to fall flat on his face and witness the fact that he could get up again and live with himself before he could think clearly about his future. Now he not only thought about it, he was looking forward to it. But first, there were a few loose ends to tie up. And Annie Kneeland was on the top of his list.

He sensed her tension. It was in her eyes, the way she took hold of her room key from the desk clerk, the funny grin she gave him when they both reached out for the elevator button at the same time.

Nick took the key from her hand and opened her door. He laughed softly as she walked in ahead of him. Annie looked over her shoulder and arched her brow.

"What's so funny?" she asked him.

"I'm not going to bite, Annie. Well, maybe just a little." He took her breath away as he grabbed her suddenly, his teeth taking nibbling bites on her neck. She gasped.

"You don't know how hungry I've been?" His voice was hotly seductive against her ear.

"How could I know—anything? I didn't even know what happened to you after Wimbledon, until I called Jeff." Her eyes reflected the hurt tone of her voice, but she didn't move out of his arms.

"Wimbledon was another century, honey. I've traveled quite a distance since then." He held her at arm's length and looked deep into her eyes. "I needed some time to get my head together. Can you understand?"

Annie nodded, the tension slipping away. She did understand. And she sensed a new beginning.

She slipped her arms around his neck and gently pressed her lips against his. She teasingly darted her tongue across his mouth, her fingers catching hold of his thick black hair. Nick lovingly cupped her face in his hands, smiling as she bit lightly, playfully, on his lower lip.

He bent slightly and lifted her up in his arms. But for a minute he didn't move. He just held her against him, relishing the sensation of having her locked in his embrace.

"I love you, Anna Falanna. My beautiful, delectible girl of my dreams. I watched you take your first step, and I am telling you now, woman,

I plan to be around for your last." He carried her to the bed. "And for all our years in between I intend to keep us both busy by making exquisite love at every opportunity." He unbuttoned her blouse, pressing his lips against her full breast and then giving her a wicked smile. "Any objections?"

"Only one." She laughed. "Stop talking and hurry up, before I ravish you. Can't you see that I'm crazy with lust?"

"I love it when you're crazy like that," he whispered, slipping her blouse off and then quickly ridding them both of the rest of their clothes.

He ran his fingers the length of her body, thrilling to the trembling sensation of her flesh. She was so beautiful and so inviting. His strong hands caressed her breasts, his lips tugging gently at her taut nipples. Annie's legs parted and he lay between them. She curled her legs around his calves, arching her back as her lips sought his.

She kissed him with a fierce desire surging through every pore of her body. She whispered her need as his lips traveled down the sensuous, elegant lines of her slender form. She cried out in ecstasy as his tongue swept a path along her inner thighs, her passion and longing growing sharper and more feverish.

He thought he knew how much he'd missed her and wanted her, but now, as she responded to his caresses, murmured his name over and over again in whispered longing and pleasure, he understood his need deep in his soul. He wrapped her tightly in his arms, kissed her with rough passion, his tongue tasting her sweetness.

Arching against him, Annie drew her hands down his back, pressing him to her with breathless urging. Nick looked down at her as he filled her body. Never had he seen a woman more beautiful. Annie's face captured a look of such joyous ecstasy that it made his heart soar. Then they both surrendered themselves to their rapturous passion.

The warm, tingling feelings continued even after Nick lay beside her, his strong body pressed against her side. He raised himself on his elbow and studied her intently. His fingers brushed her hair from her face. Annie reached up and took his hand, bringing his palm to her lips.

"Will it always be this good?" she whispered with a contented purr.

"Better. This is the kind of workout I'll never grow tired of." He grinned, leisurely skimming his hand down her side. She could feel his touch begin to arouse her again and she smiled.

"What happens now?" Annie lifted her head up against the pillow as Nick continued his sensuous meanderings.

He looked at her, his hand resting on her hip. "I've got a few more loose ends to take care of and then—"

"Loose ends?" Annie sat up higher, not noticing his hand had left her body. "What loose ends?"

"Annie, I've done a lot of thinking since Wimbledon. I was sure, when I left there with my tail between my legs, that I could never face another person across that net. But I was wrong. I was letting that one failure obscure everything I had accomplished in my career."

Annie sat up completely, pulling the covers up to her chin. She was suddenly cold, her moist skin clammy.

"Nothing has changed after all." Her voice was low, her features already growing distant, removed.

"I have to play the U.S. Open. Annie, please try to understand."

"I have tried to understand. I spent four months trying to understand. And you know what I discovered. There is no way I am ever going to accomplish that. I watched you destroy a career that you should have given up nine months ago. And now you are telling me it still isn't finished."

"Listen. It's my last chance."

"How many more last chances after that? Are you going to keep it up until you're crippled for life?"

"That won't happen if you stick by me for the next few weeks. After the U.S. Open, I—"

"You really think I could still go along with this insanity? Why I ever got into it in the first place . . ." She caught her breath. She knew why. Just as she now knew it had to stop. "On Monday I'm starting my work at St. Mead's. If you insist on destroying yourself, you're going to have to do it alone."

"Annie."

"Please go, Nick. When I saw you at the Center, I guess I fooled myself into believing we had a chance for a new beginning. But it's still the same old story with the same old, painful ending." She turned her face away from him.

Nick silently dressed. Before he left, he said softly, "You're wrong about the story, Annie. You're wrong about me."

She turned to him, tears glistening in her eyes, and she said in a voice husky with pain, "I wish I were wrong."

Nick sighed, a wistful smile curving his lips. He blew her a kiss and walked out the door. Annie was one loose end that did not tie easily, but he wasn't the kind of man who left ends hanging for long.

CHAPTER THIRTEEN

Annie walked through the hospital corridor to the orthopedic clinic. She had been working at St. Mead's for two weeks and she was beginning to feel settled. It was a good feeling; one she needed badly, given the fact that her personal life continued to be in a turmoil. She hadn't seen Nick since that evening at her hotel, but she knew he was in town practicing for the big event at Flushing Meadows because his name constantly appeared in the newspapers.

Everyone had thought Nick was through after Wimbledon. Now speculations were flying. The general consensus was he didn't stand a chance. His injury had become common knowledge. You don't tour the circuit with a personal physician unless something's up. After his disastrous defeat, with thousands of spectators watching Nick limp badly off the field at Wimbledon, there was little question about the seriousness of his condition.

Every morning she told herself she would skip the sports section of the newspaper, and every morning she read it anyway. She was still angry at Nick, but she also felt a growing sympathy for him. She thought the press was treating Nick like a lame horse who ought to be shot rather than attempt another race. Even if he was crazy to go for the U.S. Open, he certainly did not deserve the press's cynicism and harsh critiques just because his winning days were over. The public, she decided, is callous about fallen idols. They want them swept under the rug when they've lost their magnetic powers. Of course the press was still able to get mileage out of its coverage of Nick, and the ticket sales for the Open would no doubt skyrocket. One more chance to see a hero crumble and latch on to a new one.

The clinic was full as Annie stepped inside. She forced a reassuring smile for the parents and children crowding the row of seats in the waiting room. This morning's sports columns had been particularly unkind and Annie's mood reflected her irritation. If only Nick had let it go, at least the press would have let him sink quietly into oblivion.

By midmorning Annie had seen seven children and the waiting room was still full. The intense, hard work was just what she needed. She worked straight through lunch and was heading for the orthopedic ward to check on some inpatients when Bill Levitt stopped her in the hall.

Bill was the administrative head of the Orthopedic Department. He was a heavy-set man in his late thirties with a ruddy complexion, lively brown eyes only slightly subdued behind ow-lishly modern wire-rimmed glasses, and thin-ning brown hair. Annie noticed the first time she met him that he was not one of those vain men who, when they started to lose their hair, swept long strands across their scalp, protesting the reality. She could tell that Bill faced his bald-ness with casual acceptance and she respected that.

Annie liked him immediately. He had wel-comed her to St. Mead's warmly, but without being phony and effusive. She knew he was thrilled to have her on the staff. He made no bones about the fact that it was definitely an added plus not only to get a fine doctor to head their unit, but also the hefty donation from Cen-turion. Annie appreciated his honesty.

"Wherever you're rushing off to will have to wait," he said excitedly as he caught hold of her elbow. "Unless it's an emergency."

Annie smiled. "No emergency. I always rush. I do have some kids to check on upstairs, but I can give you a few minutes."

"Good. The delivery truck has just arrived with the goodies. Come down to the physical therapy ward with me and let's drool together as they unload our shiny new equipment. I still can't believe we are finally going to have some of the machines we've been trying to get our hands on for years. And we owe it all to you, Doctor."

"Annie," she corrected. "Please don't keep making a big deal over my part in this thing.

Believe me, Centurion gets a very nice write-off for this gift. Big corporations do it all the time. I'm happy to have the equipment, but let's forget about my part in it."

Bill gave her a friendly nod, but Annie knew he didn't understand. He probably thought she felt embarrassed to receive so much gratitude. She didn't care what he assumed as long as he dropped the matter. She did go down with him to watch the equipment get set up. To say St. Mead's could use it all was a complete understatement. Even with the new machines the room still could benefit from some other donations to bring their department up to top standards.

After leaving Bill downstairs she went up to the orthopedic ward as originally planned, then back to the clinic for her afternoon appointments. She didn't realize she hadn't eaten anything all day until five thirty when the clinic finally closed for the night. Stan Blumenthal and Maria Hill, two of the interns on Annie's staff, were also just finishing up with their last patients.

"What a day." Maria sighed, writing up her notes in the outer office.

Annie smiled. "What day has been different? Do you think every child in New York passes through these doors?"

Stan laughed. "It feels like it, sometimes. But then drop in on some of the other hospitals around town and you discover we only get the tip of the iceberg."

"Well, I've seen enough of the tip for one day. Vic is picking me up in his new TransAm and I plan to spend my evening luxuriating in splendor," Maria announced, closing her last folder and dropping it in the out basket. She smiled at Stan and Annie, bade them good-night, and left.

"How do you plan to spend your evening?" Stan asked. "Is somebody picking you up in his brand-new sportscar and whisking you away to a splendid penthouse for pheasant under glass?"

Annie laughed. "Not exactly. I am walking the two blocks to my apartment, and after I unpack at least a thousand boxes, I am serving myself an elegant piece of leftover chicken with whatever else I come up with in my fridge. A far cry from splendor, I'm afraid."

"I can't offer splendor. But I do know a great little French café where they can dish up something better than cold chicken and whatever." Stan paused. "That is, if you dine with underlings."

Annie looked across the room at Stan. He was an attractive man in his early twenties with naturally curly sandy-blond hair, his fair skin tanned nicely from the sun, and a lean build that carried clothes well. Even in his chinos and plaid shirt he looked good. Annie smiled. He was the perfect model of what an up-and-coming bright young doctor ought to look like.

"Does that smile mean yes, or are you softening the rejection?"

"It didn't mean either," Annie said. She really hadn't reached any decision. The offer was appealing. She was feeling lonely. The thought of facing those boxes and that cold chicken leg did not thrill her. Stan was pleasant, had a good sense of humor, and they had a lot in common. Who knew—he could even turn out to be that Mister Right she kept telling herself to be on the lookout for. At the very least, it would be a nice meal and some company for an evening.

But she had one thing on her mind—Nick. The fantasy of riding off in the sunset, for one night or a lifetime, with a potential Mister Right somehow didn't hold much weight. So much for fantasies. The only ones she still couldn't shake were those about Nick.

"I'm sorry, Stan. I think I'd better take a rain check. I've got—some things on my mind right now."

Stan accepted the brush-off with a good-natured smile. He happened to follow tennis closely and he knew that Nick Winters and Annie had spent the last four months together. It was not difficult to figure out just what was on her mind. He picked up his briefcase, patting it.

"You're forcing me to face all of this paperwork, now that I have no excuse for procrastinating."

"See, I'm doing us both a service. When we each have our house in order, I'd enjoy trying that café of yours."

"Then, I'll be very diligent," he said, giving her a charming smile.

As Stan walked out the door, Annie sighed.

She had a feeling there were going to be a lot more nights of cold chicken awaiting her.

The orthopedic unit was in a small wing on the north end of the hospital. It could be entered from the main lobby, or through a courtyard, where there was a cordoned-off parking area for the use of the clinic staff. Annie usually used the courtyard entrance because it was a shortcut to and from her apartment. As she neared the parking area, she spotted Nick's Porsche immediately. This time he couldn't take her reserved space, since she didn't use a car for work, so he'd pulled into Harry Williamson's spot. Today was Harry's day off so he couldn't object, but Annie most definitely did. This was one déjà vu experience she had no desire to relive.

"Don't tell me. Nick Winters's in my office," Annie cut off the secretary as she walked briskly down the hall directly to the door marked Dr. Anne Kneeland.

"You're in the wrong seat," she snapped at him as she stepped inside her office. "If you want to replay a scene, then do it right. I guess having to park in some other doctor's reserved spot must have thrown you. I don't think Dr. Williamson is going to understand or be pleased by your little rerun."

"Dr. Williamson isn't in today. I was given permission by the secretary to use his parking spot. And, as you so accurately observed, I've

242

taken the patient's seat, not the esteemed doctor's throne."

She looked at him, still angry but somewhat
deflated. "I'm not your doctor anymore. My
contract's up." Her words were strong, but her
voice lacked conviction. The Hyppocratic oath
says nothing about contractual agreements.

"I'm not here for treatment," Nick said softly,
standing up.

"No." The word exploded from her lips. She
backed up, shaking her head from side to side.
"No," she said again, with equal force. As Nick
walked toward her, she repeated it a third time.
I'm not about to lose my mind again, she kept
telling herself. I'm tired of saying good-bye and
crying in my pillow and wishing you'd climb
into my bed and make love to me, and then I
end up saying good-bye again. No, no, no.

She didn't have to say the words out loud for
Nick to interpret the meaning of her vociferous
no's. He had no trouble reading her mind. Still,
he walked over to her despite her protests and
withdrawal, gave her a brief kiss, a smile, and
told her not to go anywhere. Then he was out
the door like a flash. Annie stood where she was,
too stunned to move.

She was still standing exactly where he'd left
her when he returned. A tall, lanky boy with
unruly black hair and distrustful gray eyes followed Nick inside. Nick caught the boy's elbow
and pushed him into the forefront.

"Baker, meet Dr. Kneeland. Don't be nervous. She only uses her special hypodermic needle on those near and dear to her."

"I ain't afraid of no needles," he muttered, his eyes narrowing. "This is the chick you were falling all over at the Center."

Annie recognized Baker, too. He was the kid who had shouted at Nick to stop making time with her and get back to work.

"Now, Baker. The doctor, here, is very professional. We don't call her 'chick' on her turf. And I think that's going some to say I was falling all over her that day. I was simply making plans to make time with her later. I keep telling you, man. You've got a lot to learn."

"Do you two mind if I get a word in, or should I just go about my business and leave you to volley back and forth?" Annie looked from Nick to Baker and back to Nick again.

"I told you, Baker. She's very serious about her work. Tell her about your leg."

"Aw, will you forget it, Nick? I didn't want to come here today. I had enough of doctors and hospitals. There ain't anything you're going to do for me," he said to Annie.

"Suppose you let me be the judge of that."

Baker made some kind of snarling remark that Annie couldn't interpret. She knew Nick was roping her in, but she had to admit there was something about Baker, behind all the cool bravado and slick talk, that had her interest.

Nick translated, or rather he provided the answer to why he had brought Baker to see her.

"Baker's got this problem with his leg. Five

years ago it got broken in about a dozen places, thanks to one of our wonderful city drivers. Baker's mother was on welfare; the kid was taken to a city hospital and they tried to put his leg back together. It left Baker with a fair limp, but as far as the hospital was concerned, they had accomplished their task. Any further corrective surgery they considered elective. Only, Baker's mom didn't have the moola to elect anything."

Annie looked from Nick to Baker. The boy was staring at Nick with undisguised adoration until he caught Annie's eye. Then he immediately drew on his tough, cool mask and stared down at his torn sneakers.

"The thing is," Nick continued, "Baker here is the biggest tennis natural I've ever seen—next to me, of course." He grinned. "On one bum leg he can wipe the courts with every other kid at the Center. He could probably whip quite a few semipros. With two legs going for him, there is no stopping the guy. He could go straight to the top. All I'm asking you to do is tell us whether that leg of his could be mended further. He deserves a chance, and I don't know anyone else who believes that more than you do," he added, giving her one of his sweetly earnest smiles.

Nick had not only roped her in, he had tied a firm knot. Annie shook her head in resignation, her blue eyes flashing. "Go wait outside and let me talk to Baker." Annie issued her order pointing to the door. Nick grinned, gave Baker a supportive pat on the back, and sauntered out.

Before he closed the door he turned to the boy. "Take it easy, Baker. She's the best."

Baker looked doubtful—and scared. Behind the tough-guy act was a frightened boy. Annie did not doubt that he had had his fill of hospitals and pain.

"You have a first name, Baker?" Her tone was friendly, but not chummy enough to make him balk.

"David. Nobody calls me that except my mother."

Annie got the message. "How old are you?"

"What difference does it make? Are you going to check my leg or not?"

"Do you want me to?"

"No. Yeah. I don't know."

"That covers the whole spectrum."

He gave her a funny look. She would have to keep her vocabulary in line with his.

"I'll look at your leg."

"I'm thirteen."

"You look older."

Baker smiled. It faded when Annie told him to take off his clothes and put on a gown behind the screen. "I ain't wearing one of those things. No way. I never even put one of them on when I was in the hospital."

"How do I check your leg out, then?" Annie asked, feeling for David Baker's embarrassment as well as his need to preserve his macho cool, especially when he was feeling so vulnerable. For a moment he reminded her of Nick.

Baker had come prepared. Despite his ambivalence about seeing another doctor, Annie realized the boy had total trust in Nick and if Nick wanted Annie to examine him, he would go along with it. Under his well-worn dungarees he wore a pair of tennis shorts. They were new, still crisply white. Annie figured they were a gift from Nick.

"I'm going to do a preliminary exam and then take some X rays. I need to see how your bones healed after your accident. Okay?" As she looked at David sitting on the edge of the exam table, trying desperately to appear cool, she felt it was very important to put him at ease by explaining to him exactly what was going to be happening. She had told him before that he looked older than thirteen. Now, sitting there on the table swinging his legs back and forth and pushing his dark hair out of his eyes, he seemed much younger. And, Annie thought, more appealing. She could understand why Nick had been drawn to him. It was not only the boy's talent, but something about David Baker himself. Annie felt it, too.

"Do you ever get pain in that leg?" Annie asked as she began her exam. David was very quiet.

"No. Well, maybe sometimes. Ma says it's because the weather is bad. She says she always knows when it's gonna rain cause I start to limp more that day. Most times nobody notices I got a gimp leg."

Annie nodded. David's voice had lost its hardness. He was a young boy who had suffered a great deal of pain, physically and emotionally. In the kind of environment David lived in, it was important to be strong and whole. A gimp leg, as he called it, would no doubt be the butt of a lot of hurtful teasing. But David clearly had a special kind of strength and determination and he had fought many years of his young life against the stigma.

"I must admit, I didn't notice you limp when you came in."

David smiled. He had a sweet, natural smile that softened the tough mask he usually wore. "That's because the sun is shining."

Annie laughed. "Moms are pretty smart."

"So what's with you and Winters?" David blurted out as Annie continued her exam.

"I don't think I follow your question, Baker." Now it was Annie's turn to feel uptight.

"Come on. You two got a thing going?"

Annie paused. She looked at David carefully, sensing at once that he was not trying to be fresh or cocky. He seemed to need to know where she stood with Nick.

"You like the guy, huh?" Annie observed.

"Winters? He's the best." He flushed and then grinned. "You think so, too?"

Annie grinned. "He's okay."

"Come off it. I seen the way you check him out. You think he's more than okay."

"If you know so much, Baker, why are you giving me the third degree?" Annie tousled his hair affectionately. Ten minutes ago David

248

would have bristled at that touch. Now he merely grinned.

"Hey, watch the locks. I work hard to get a special look, you know what I mean?"

"Oh, yes, Baker. I know just what you mean."

"So, what next?"

"I'm going to X-ray—"

"No, I mean with you and Nick. You gonna shack up together or get married or something?" He looked at her intently.

Annie shook her head and smiled. "Forget tennis, Baker. You ought to go in for law."

"You don't know yet, huh?"

"You are wise beyond your years, David Baker. I don't know yet," Annie said frankly.

David smiled sagely. They waited together in comfortable, shared silence for the X rays. When they came back, Annie clipped them to the illuminated panel and studied them for a couple of minutes.

"Shall I ask Nick to come back in?"

"Yeah." David's voice had a catch in it. This was it. He was either going to live with this limp forever or be given a chance to be healed completely.

Nick came in and stood next to David, his hand casually resting on the boy's shoulder. Annie stood a little off to the side, closer to the X rays.

"What do you think, Annie?" Nick asked, keeping his voice light and easy. If it was no-go, he had to help David get through it without losing face. Not to mention his own feeling of guilt for dragging the boy down only to be told things were hopeless.

"There's a chance," Annie said slowly, looking at them both. "A small chance that if we operate we might be able to correct some of the areas that never knit back properly. There's no guarantee it would completely solve the problem." Now she looked straight at David. "You might improve, but the damaged leg could still be shorter than the other. The limp would be better, but not necessarily gone."

David swallowed hard, but didn't answer.

"Is there a chance you could correct the damage so the kid didn't have any limp at all?" Nick asked.

Annie noticed Nick's hand squeezing the boy's shoulder.

"There's a chance," she said softly. "I can't really know until we see the damage firsthand. It could be worse than I think."

"But you think there's a chance?" Nick persisted.

"David, I have to be as clear with you as possible. This operation means more pain, more hospital time," Annie said straightforwardly, "and more hassles with doctors."

"You'd be head man, right?"

Annie nodded.

"Then, I can handle it."

Nick patted David on the back. "Buddy, maybe you should think about it a little. Annie's putting it to you straight. It's going to hurt and there are no guarantees."

"Hey, man, I ain't never played good odds. The doc here says I got a chance. You think I shouldn't take it?"

Nick gazed at David as the boy stared back. There was such a tight bond there that Annie could almost touch it. In an amazingly short time Nick had reached out to David and captured his heart. He had also given his own.

"There are always risks in life, friend. You have to take the ones that matter the most." Nick looked from David to Annie. It was a message he wanted them both to hear.

Annie looked into Nick's eyes and nodded slowly.

There was more than one bond in that room. New ones and old filled the air.

David told Annie he was sure he wanted to go through with the surgery. As soon as possible, he emphasized. Annie explained she would need to speak with David's mother and get her permission. She wasn't sure how to bring up the issue of cost. Mrs. Baker's welfare check wouldn't be able to cover the cost of the medication, never mind the hospital bills. Annie had already decided she would not charge for her services, but that still left the rest—which she knew would be substantial.

David retrieved his cool, tough mask, and after thanking her, he left. Nick stayed behind.

Annie slipped the X rays back in the envelope. "I like your protégé," she said to Nick.

"I thought you would. He reminds me a lot of Jeff when I first met him." Nick leaned against the wall and watched Annie busy herself rear-ranging files on her desk.

She stopped. "That's funny. He reminded me more of you."

"Me?"

"That cool, casual, tough-guy image—fast talking, glib. Even similar dark good looks. And underneath"—she looked into his eyes—"underneath the façade is a gentle vulnerability and deep, intense feelings."

Nick couldn't remember the last time he had blushed, but he could feel his face begin to redden. "I wish you understood how deeply I do feel."

"I do understand, Nick."

The only problem was Nick was talking about Annie and Annie was talking about tennis.

She changed the subject. Her understanding did not ease her pain. "Have you thought about how Mrs. Baker is going to pay for David's operation?"

"I'll take care of the costs."

"Nick, your medical insurance isn't going to cover David. We're talking about thousands of dollars. And if there are complications . . ."

Nick walked over to Annie and took hold of her hands. "Weren't you the woman who told me I ought to start doing something constructive with all my money?"

Annie smiled. "I think I remember the speech."

"I've been giving that speech a lot of careful

thought. Maybe we could have dinner tonight and I can tell you about some of my ideas."

Annie stepped back. "I'm—I'm busy tonight and you're in training. We're only going to end up in some kind of an argument. You can't afford that again. And to be honest, neither can I."

"We don't have to fight, Annie." His dark eyes glistened with a seductive warmth.

Annie turned away. "Nick, don't make things harder. Hopping back in bed with you is a very temporary solution to our problems."

"Not if you would stop hopping out all the time." He moved close to her again as he saw her resistance start to melt. Her eyes pleaded with him to understand her, but even she wasn't certain what she was pleading for—or what she wanted.

Stan Blumenthal walked in as Nick was about to kiss Annie.

"Sorry. I—I thought you were in between appointments." This was a day for blushing. Both Stan's and Annie's faces glowed with rosy hues. Nick merely wore a frown and cursed the intruder's lousy timing.

"I am," Annie said emphatically. "I'll let you know when I make all the arrangements for David's surgery," she muttered quickly to Nick. "I have to get back to work now."

"Sure," Nick said, the seductive note still in his voice. "Give me a call when you're ready."

Nick smiled as her cheeks reddened again.

"Thanks," he added, before he nodded to Stan and left.

Annie tried to compose herself as Stan talked with her about one of his patients. He was very sensitive and went on for a while letting her gather her thoughts together. Finally, they were able to discuss the case constructively and Stan was pleased with Annie's observations.

"You know your stuff, Doctor," Stan praised. "I'll follow through on your suggestions." He tapped the folder in his hand, lingering.

"Is there something else you wanted to talk to me about?"

"This is probably the wrong time to ask, but something tells me you could use a good meal tonight. And a good friend."

"You know something, Stan? You're right on both accounts."

CHAPTER FOURTEEN

Marion Baker walked into the office. She was a small woman with a once-pretty face, worn by time and hard luck. Her drab cotton housedress added to the picture of a woman who had always viewed the system from the bottom looking up. But her short dark hair, neatly brushed, and the gray eyes, like David's but lacking that wary caution, showed another side of Marion Baker. Her eyes were warm, shining with life despite many hardships, and she had put her best effort into her appearance.

Annie extended her hand to David's mother. Mrs. Baker smiled. Her smile startlingly transformed her face, making her at once younger and prettier. Annie saw where David got his looks.

"David is very excited, Doctor. He wants this operation very badly. I—I want him to have it, if that's what he wants. He's been through so much. Not only the accident with his leg, but a lot of things. No father, no money, no decent clothes, a couple of times no roof over his head to speak of. Since Mr. Winters took an interest in David and got him so involved down at the Center, it's been almost a miracle, the change in the boy. He goes around smiling, he's stopped hanging out at pool halls—why, he practically lives over at the Center. And talks about Mr. Winters night and day."

"I think they have a mutual admiration society going between the two of them." Annie smiled.

"I think so, too. Mr. Winters sure must care a lot to be willing to pay for the operation. I felt real funny about that at first, but what other choice do I have? Could I say no to my son because of my pride? No, Doctor. I learned years ago, pride don't buy food or pay the rent."

"The only pride you ought to concern yourself with, Mrs. Baker, is the pride you can rightly feel in your son. He's a fine young boy."

"You know the most wonderful thing about all of this? Until Mr. Winters and Mr. and Mrs. Reese came along, and now you, too, Doctor Kneeland, there haven't been any people beside me who could see through to the soul of my boy." Mrs. Baker caught her breath, briskly wiping away her tears.

Annie blinked a few times, too.

"I'm very grateful to you all," she murmured. "My boy has a real chance for the first time in his life to make something of himself. 'Cause for the first time he really wants to." She could no longer hold back her tears and pressed her palms tightly against her eyes, sobbing quietly.

Annie handed her some tissues and took a handful for herself.

She knew she should explain to Mrs. Baker that her son's operation might not do all she hoped, but Annie couldn't get it out. Somehow she had to make it happen—for David, his mother, Nick—and for herself.

Stan was careful with his opinion. "You know better than I do, Annie, that these cases can be mighty tricky. Especially after a five-year period."

The cheerful Chinese waiter whisked away the porcelain bowls of finished wonton soup, immediately replacing them with two steaming bowls of white rice and a small, oval stainless-steel-covered casserole.

This was the second dinner Annie had eaten with Stan this week. The first had been pure friendship and this one was one part friendship and nine parts business. Annie wanted Stan to assist in David Baker's operation and their discussion of David's case had moved from the office to the Chinese restaurant.

From the moment Stan had walked in on Annie and Nick in that near embrace in her office, he was aware of the score. The fact that Annie never mentioned Nick since then convinced Stan all the more that Annie was far from having her house in order. If he were a betting man, he would have put his money on Nick. Annie's resistance was hanging by a thread. He would have liked to come up with a way to alter the situation. Annie Kneeland was not only brilliant, successful, and gorgeous. She was also a warm, sensitive woman with a queen-sized heart. Unfortunately, her heart clearly belonged to Nick, even if she refused to recognize it.

Annie served Stan some Yu Tsang broccoli and then took some for herself. Deftly, she lifted up a tender stem of the vegetable with her chopsticks and brought it to her lips.

Stan smiled. "I'm impressed. That's why you're a first-class surgeon. Terrifically fine motor coordination."

"I think we stand a good chance," Annie said, bringing the conversation back to David. "Five years is a long time, but the X rays looked promising."

Stan arched a brow.

"All right," she confessed, "that's an exaggeration. But they didn't rule out success."

"Annie, if anyone can do it, I believe you can." He hesitated.

"Go on, Stan. Tell me what you're thinking. We're friends, not just colleagues, right?"

"Look, Annie, I may be completely out of line, but you asked me to tell you what's on my mind, so I will. If Nick Winters wasn't involved in this case, I don't think you would be sitting here trying desperately to convince yourself that you are going to perform miracles no matter what the odds."

"That's not true," she protested angrily.

"See, I told you I was probably out of line."

"You think I'm spinning fairy tales?" she asked less defensively.

"I think you're longing for a fairy-tale ending, and I sure as hell hope you find it. But real life doesn't always have that happy ending."

"I've discovered that enough times," Annie admitted.

"Are you talking about you and Nick Winters?"

Annie frowned, on the defense again.

"I seem to be getting in the habit of stepping out of line with you. Sorry. You don't have to tell me it's none of my business. I know." He gave her a wan smile.

"Nick Winters is a subject I try my best to avoid thinking about. I'm never very successful. You're right about my feeling desperate about the Baker boy. Partly it has to do with Nick. But it's gone deeper than that. I feel something special for David. He's a fighter—tough, strong, independent. I have this sense that he could do so much with his life given the chance. I don't particularly want to see him become a tennis superstar like Nick, but I think if the operation is a success it will give David the self-confidence to do anything he wants."

"We'll keep our fingers crossed," Stan said with a warm smile.

"Not during the operation, however," Annie said with a grin.

Nick's eyes kept shifting to the large clock on the wall. They shouldn't have clocks in hospital waiting rooms, he decided. It was dreadful watching the hands move so slowly, feeling time stand still. Annie had said the operation would take at least a couple of hours, maybe more if there were complications. Nick hated the word —"complications." When Annie had said it, he'd felt a black, heavy cloud drop over him. No complications, he prayed silently.

Marion Baker sipped black coffee, refusing to look at the clock even once. She knew all about time standing still. Five years ago she'd sat for what had felt like a lifetime in another room similar to this one, waiting to hear whether her son's leg could be saved. And then she'd experienced an unbelievable feeling of relief after learning that his leg would not have to be amputated.

Staring out the window, Marion Baker wondered if she would ever be able to erase from her mind the sound of that first awful shriek— squealing tires and the piercing wail of excruciating pain. Her boy, so little and defenseless, lying in the street, his leg mangled beneath him. She took a deep gulp of the hot liquid. No matter what happened this time, her boy was okay. The accident had not only left scars, it had left David stronger and more determined. He had learned to be a fighter. And, she thought, looking around at Jeff and Barbara, and then at Nick, her boy had made some good friends. Again she remembered that other long, lonely wait. That day she had been all alone. Today was different. Marion felt a comforting sense of well-being. Yes, she thought, no matter what happens, things are different now.

"Can I get you something to eat, hon?" Jeff gave his wife a worried look. She had been too nervous about the operation to eat breakfast and it was nearing lunchtime. No one wanted to leave the waiting room to go to the cafeteria, in case there was any news.

Barbara gave Jeff a reassuring squeeze. "In a little while. Maybe Mrs. Baker would like a sandwich or another cup of coffee. Or Nick?"

They both shook their heads, no.

"You should eat something," Marion Baker insisted. "I remember when I was pregnant with David, I used to get real dizzy if I skipped meals. I guess that was his way of letting me know I'd better feed him. He still eats like a horse, that boy."

They all smiled. At the Center they had seen David wolf down huge quantities of food from the little snack bar Barbara had set up. She had run it until recently, when Jeff insisted she stay off her feet until the baby came.

When the two-hour mark passed nobody said a word. But the mood in the small, confined room took on a more oppressive atmosphere. Barbara had forced herself to take a few bites of a cheese sandwich for Jeff's sake, but she couldn't muster up any appetite. The other three didn't even bother to try to eat. Marion drank three more cups of black coffee, Jeff chewed on some Life Savers, and Nick kept trying not to watch the clock.

When Annie walked into the room an hour later, Jeff and Barbara were holding hands, staring at the door. Nick looked up and met her eyes. He reached over and took hold of Marion Baker's hand.

As soon as they all saw her, they knew it hadn't gone well. Annie's face mirrored the pain she felt deep in the pit of her stomach. She had done everything possible, but David's leg had simply suffered too much damage to do anything more than slightly improve his limp. David Baker would never have the opportunity to decide whether or not he wanted to become the super tennis star Nick believed he could be. That decision had been made for him on the operating table that day.

Marion Baker was the first to speak. "I know you did your best, Dr. Kneeland."

"I'm afraid my best wasn't enough," she whispered. "I wanted to make his leg perfect again. I know how much he wanted to be given the chance to become a pro tennis player someday. I'm afraid that is one area that will probably always be closed to him. I'm sorry."

Nick, more than anyone else knew that David had nurtured secret dreams for years about being a famous athlete. To a poor kid with few opportunities for ways out of the ghetto, sports was one door that was open to someone with talent. When David had discovered his ability in tennis, he had begun to let himself believe he could follow in Nick's footsteps. If his own footsteps could ever be corrected, that is. Nick could physically feel the door shut as Annie stood looking at them all.

He walked over to her. "I'd like to tell him. I'm the one that started this whole thing. Encouraging his fantasies, making him believe they could come true. It's all my fault."

"He's under heavy sedation, Nick. Talk with him tomorrow, when his head is clear and he—he . . . excuse me," she whispered, the tears slipping down her cheeks. She hurried out of the room.

Nick came after her, pulling her over to a corner of the hallway.

"I was the one that was wrong, Nick," Annie told him. "I let my wishes get in the way of my professional judgment. I shouldn't have offered hope. I should have—"

"Hold on, Annie. Don't put the blame on yourself. You never said, not once, that the chances were anything but slim. David understood that and he was willing to take the risk."

"I know. I know. But I wanted—I wanted to work miracles. Only, I couldn't. I'm just a plain doctor."

"You're just human. It hurts to fail even when you give it your best shot."

She looked at him long and hard. "But maybe there are times when you have to quit when you're ahead."

"You're still in there plugging, aren't you?" He smiled. "Don't worry, Anna Falanna. I plan to quit when I'm ahead. But first, I am going to win the U.S. Open for David, and he and I are both going to end up winners."

"Oh, Nick . . ."

"Annie." He reached up and lifted her chin so that their eyes met. "Let me take you home. This is not the time for fighting."

"Don't worry, Nick. I think all the fight's been knocked out of me today."

They walked hand in hand back to the waiting room. Marion had gone into the recovery room to sit by her son. Barbara told Annie that David's mother seemed to be handling this better than any of them.

Barbara put her arms around Annie. "Being a bigshot athlete is no great shakes. We two know that better than most."

"We know it, but I think it's not going to be an easy task convincing David of that reality. From his perspective the life of a superstar has to look pretty damn good."

Annie also believed that David's desire to be like his mentor ran very deep and the sharp pangs of disappointment were feelings both David and Nick would probably experience for a long time to come. Nick was going to take his disappointment out on the tennis court at the U.S. Open. How was David going to cope with his?

Nick knew when he took Annie home from the hospital that he wouldn't be leaving that night. Annie knew it, too. Tomorrow would come soon enough and for all Annie's arguments about hating the painful endings, she seemed only capable of thinking about today. And today she needed Nick desperately. She wanted him to wrap his love and caring around her in a warm, safe cocoon. Today they needed each other, even though tomorrow would bring another painful good-bye.

The fight was out of her, but not her feeling of futility about any future with Nick. With everything that had happened today, Nick seemed more determined than ever to work out all of his emotions on the tennis court.

Still, it didn't matter at this moment. As they walked into her apartment and he pressed her tightly to him, Annie forgot about tennis and tomorrows and everything else except the feeling that, in his arms, she was home once again.

Nick drew her head up to him, gazing intently at her face. He saw all the strain and exhaustion that she had felt that day in her eyes. He felt the echo of her need and the new bond that had formed between them in their shared feelings for a young boy now lying in a lonely hospital bed. Nick captured a wayward tear as it trickled down her cheek.

His touch was her release and his. They held each other knowing that their tears were for so many lost dreams and wishes they were unable to make come true. Fate always seemed to bring their paths together and then force them apart. And this, too, was yet another meeting in a storm, and when the storm subsided they would go their separate ways again.

But today they held each other, giving love and comfort, compassion and strength. Nick lay beside her on her bed, tenderly running his hand along her dark hair, letting the silken strands slip through his fingers. He softly whispered her name and she curled against him, her body curving into his so perfectly. His strong arms encircled her, his breathy kisses along the nape of her neck and across her shoulders making her tremble.

"I love you, Annie." His voice caressed her. "I love what you tried to do today. I love the depth of your compassion. I love your heart and soul," he said as he pressed his lips against her breast, "and I love your warm, inviting body."

With a bittersweet surrender Annie reached up and drew him on top of her. When they were together like this, safe from the world outside, nothing else mattered but loving and being loved. She arched her back as he pressed deep inside of her, her gasp of pleasure meeting his as Nick's mouth covered hers in tender passion.

Later, as the sun went down, they lay together on top of the sheets in relaxed contentment. Annie watched the shadow of the setting sun dancing across the white walls of her room. Nick's eyes fell on Annie's long, slender body. He studied the way her hair spread over his shoulder as she nestled against him. He lovingly followed the gentle swell of her ribcage as her breaths came slow and easy now. He closed his eyes envisioning her face in that exquisite moment when he had brought her to ecstasy. He could almost feel again the taut shuddering motion of her body as she reached the point of fulfillment and then the utter abandonment with which she gave herself up to the release.

In the darkness that surrounded the room, their silent thoughts returned again to David.

"Will he be all right, Nick?"

It didn't surprise him that her thoughts had traveled to the same place as his. They were so connected tonight he assumed their minds as well as their bodies had joined together.

"He's an amazing kid. When I first met him he was so tough and street-wise. He kind of accepted me because he trusted Jeff and Barbara. We played a game of tennis. He gave me quite a run for my money, I'll tell you." He laughed. "Right from the start I sensed something in this kid that was special. And after that game we both found ourselves communicating as though—as though we had somehow always known each other. For some reason I still don't understand we not only saw behind each other's defenses, neither of us felt scared about it."

"David thinks you are the greatest guy in the world," Annie said with a smile.

"He might not, after tomorrow." Nick stared up at the ceiling. "He might hate me for getting his hopes up about all of this."

"You were the one who pointed out to me that David accepted the odds and was willing to take the risk anyway. Nick, he hasn't lost anything he had before this operation."

"He's lost a dream," Nick said in a whisper.

"There are other dreams," Annie said, slipping her hand in his. Oh, can't you see, Nick, there can be other dreams for anyone willing to reach up and grab them, her silent thoughts cried out. But she knew it was futile to say the words out loud. Nick had believed all his life in only one dream and one path, and the time for grabbing new ones seemed to have passed him by.

Later that night, after they had eaten some dinner, they walked together back to the hospital. Marion Baker had finally gone home a couple of hours before. David was still under heavy sedation. Nick and Annie looked down at the sleeping boy, so much a child in his slumber. Gently, Nick reached out and took hold of David's hand. In his sleep David tightened the grip.

CHAPTER FIFTEEN

Time magazine's cover showed a split screen photo of Nick Winters and Seth Colliston, each poised in that final moment of victory at the U.S. Open semifinals matches in Flushing Meadows. WILL THIS BE THE YEAR OF THE NEW YOUNG BREED?

A few weeks ago most sportswriters wouldn't have even bothered to pose the question. But Nick Winters, given up for lost, had seemingly risen from the ashes of failure, coming through the matches at Flushing Meadows with a vengeance. Tomorrow he would once again face his most powerful opponent across the court, and despite the fact that Colliston was still the number-one pick, general consensus was that Winters might just pull off this win after all.

Annie had the magazine in her hand as she walked into the hospital that morning. She had intentionally avoided Nick since the day after David's operation ten days ago. Nick had been in to see David every chance he could, given his tight schedule at the Open, but Annie had made sure she was busily involved whenever Nick stopped by to say hello. She was making every effort to avoid any scenes or arguments. Too much was at stake and Annie did not want to recreate another Wimbledon by having any more big blowups with Nick. The likelihood of that blowup rose every time she watched him trying not to limp off the courts after a match.

Several times during the past ten days Annie had spoken with Mac on the phone. They were both worried about Nick's ankle, especially as Nick had refused any other medical intervention or care. Bill Kenny was back wrapping the Ace bandages. Annie was relieved when Mac told her Nick was not taking any pain-killers during the matches, but she and Mac both knew that with each game, Nick was heading closer to the possibility of seriously reinjuring that ankle.

David Baker had been groggy with pain the first few days after the surgery. Annie knew Nick had spoken with him for over an hour the day after the operation, but David was close-mouthed about that conversation. Annie could not tell whether or not Nick had been able to ease the boy's disappointment.

Whenever Annie dropped by, David seemed to make a rigorous effort to be cheerful, in that cool, tough-guy style he had learned so well. It was as though he was more concerned about her feelings of failure than he was about his own situation.

Mrs. Baker was coming out of David's room when Annie approached. "I just brought David some clothes. He's real excited. I guess after ten days feeling stir crazy he's mighty glad to be coming home. And I have to admit, the house has been too quiet without him. I even miss picking up his clothes and sneakers he constantly leaves scattered all over the place. Don't tell him that, though." Marion Baker smiled.

"I won't," Annie assured her. They walked down the hall together. "Can I ask you something, Mrs. Baker?"

David's mother nodded.

"Tell me honestly. How do you think David is feeling about what's happened? He always tried to give me the impression that it's no big deal. But I know he has to have some strong emotions about the operation not being a success."

Marion Baker looked at Annie. "David's always kept his feelings to himself, Dr. Kneeland. Even when he was in the hospital that first time, do you know he never cried. Not once. A long while after, I finally asked him how come he never did cry. He was only eight years old, mind you, when he was hit by that car. You know what he told me?" Mrs. Baker paused, taking a deep breath. "He told me he couldn't cry because he knew how sad it would make me feel. And he was the man of the family, he said, so he had to be strong and look after me—even—even if he did only have one good leg to stand on."

Marion Baker coughed in embarrassment as she dabbed away at her tears. "I guess I cry enough for both of us." She managed a smile. "Don't you worry about David, Dr. Kneeland.

He'll work this through. One thing the Bakers know how to do is face life and keep going."

Annie turned to Marion Baker and gave her a tight hug. "I once told you I thought you had a very special son. I forgot to say that David has a very special mother."

Flushed, but with a warm, pleased smile also lighting up her face, Marion Baker whispered her thanks and said good-bye. "Oh, I almost forgot. David asked if you would go in to see him before he goes home this afternoon."

"I was on my way there," Annie said, "when I saw you. I'll go right over now." She turned to go and then looked back at David's mother for a moment. "Marion, thanks. I'll see you next week when you bring David in for his follow-up appointment."

Annie's step was lighter as she walked toward David's room. She knocked softly on the door and heard a cheerful voice telling her to come in.

David was sitting in the green vinyl hospital chair, his left leg propped up on the stool. He was wearing a pair of white tennis shorts and a T-shirt with the name REC CENTER in bold red lettering across the front. Annie felt her heart sink as she saw him. Without that cast wrapped around his leg he looked the perfect picture of a young tennis player. She took a deep breath and put on a smile.

"How's it going?" she asked lightly.

David grinned. "Pretty good. Pretty good."

Annie walked over to him and looked down at

the cast, inscribed with dozens of samples of handwriting.

"I don't know if you should read all of this. Some of it is kind of X rated." He grinned. "A lot of the guys from the Rec Center have put their words of wisdom on here for me. To kind of boost my spirits, you know what I mean?"

Annie nodded. "And have they?"

"Hey," David exclaimed, ignoring Annie's question, "you didn't put your John Hancock on my cast. Come on, you gotta write something."

Annie stared down at the cast. "I—I . . ."

"Don't be shy. You could write something like, 'To the greatest-looking guy this side of East Eighteenth Street, Best Wishes from the woman who is really mad about you!' Or something like that." He grinned sheepishly. "If you weren't Nick's woman, I'd try to make you see I'd be worth waiting for. Give me a few years, and . . ."

Annie laughed. "Watch it, Baker. This *conversation* is getting X rated. Give me a pen."

Annie bent down and wrote, "To David Baker, if I were a few years younger . . ." And then she added a P.S. "I wish you new dreams, new hopes, and a long joyful life fulfilling them. You are a very special star. Love, Annie."

David bit intently at his lower lip as he read Annie's words. As she stood up, he said, "Don't feel bad. I know you're bummed out cause you didn't get this leg of mine all straightened out."

"I'm so sorry, David. I know how much it meant to you to have the opportunity to be a great tennis pro like Nick. I know how much it meant to him, too. It mustn't seem fair to you. I know, plenty of times, it doesn't seem fair to me."

"You got it wrong," he reassured her. "Sure, I thought it might be neat living it up as a big-time athlete. I'm pretty damn good with a racket, if I say so myself. But—but that's never been the really big thing. Not as big as—as having a friend like Nick Winters. And Jeff and Barbara. You, too." He winked. "Winters has good taste."

Annie laughed. "In friends, too."

David grabbed his crutches and stood up. He walked over to the window. Looking outside, he said in a low voice, "I never knew my dad. He—he ran out on my mom before I hit town. I don't have any brothers, and for a long time I figured I was best off being a kind of loner. I always thought everybody was out for something in this world. There's always an angle. Only, Nick taught me that wasn't true. He showed me people can care."

He turned around to face Annie. "You know what I was most scared about when I found out the operation didn't work. I was scared, if I couldn't be a tennis pro like Nick, maybe— maybe he wouldn't want anything much to do with me."

"Oh, David, Nick isn't like that. He cares—"

"You don't have to tell me. I know. Nick has really been here for me. And you want to hear something funny? He was scared, too. He told me he was afraid I'd drop out of the program and never want anything to do with him anymore. Can you believe that? He was really worried I wouldn't want to be his friend. Jeez, he's the best friend a guy could have."

Annie closed her eyes, fighting back her tears. David looked out the window again and continued talking.

"Yesterday, when Nick came up to see me, we had a real long talk about what I was going to do with my life. He's really on my case. Wants me to take the time to think about all the possibilities I got going for me. He thinks I'm a pretty smart dude. He feels bad, he told me, that he fell into sports when he was too young to know the price he was gonna pay. He said in a way, this bum leg of mine wasn't so bad. I mean, I may not be able to be a big-time athlete, but outside of that, I guess Nick's right. I can do anything. I can reach for any star, like Nick says. You know what else he—he's gonna do?"

Annie looked up as she heard the catch in David's throat. Tears were falling down the boy's cheeks, but he seemed oblivious of them.

Annie walked closer to him. David smiled through his tears. "Nick told me he's gonna take half of his winnings tomorrow and put them in a trust fund for me—for my college education, he said. Can you believe that guy? He's the greatest." David sniffed loudly and blew his nose into the tissue Annie handed him. She was glad she had an extra one for herself.

When David managed to get his voice back, he said huskily, "Nick gave me two tickets to the finals match tomorrow. You want—you want to go with me and watch our man win?"

Without hesitation Annie smiled, and nodded yes. Tears glistened on her cheeks and her sea-blue eyes held, at last, a profound understanding of the man she so deeply loved. For the first time she truly believed that she and Nick would be winners along with David, no matter what happened at Flushing Meadows tomorrow.

As Annie started toward the door, David called out to her. She looked back at him.

"I was just wondering. What do you think about my becoming a lawyer or something like that? Were you joking that day you told me I ought to consider it?"

"I think you'd make a terrific lawyer, David. You'd make a terrific anything for that matter," Annie said with a great big smile.

Mac watched Nick wind up his practice session. His eyes stayed focused particularly on Nick's footwork. After the semifinals match Nick's ankle had swelled badly. Mac had tried to get him to go see Annie, but Nick had vehemently refused. He was as scared as Annie at this point of any confrontations. He needed every ounce of energy and stamina to see the tournament through. He had never blamed Annie for having affected his loss at Wimbledon, but Nick knew that all his fight had to be saved for the tennis court. If Annie had taken a look at that messed-up ankle sparks would definitely have started flying.

"How do you feel?" Mac asked as Nick joined him back in the locker room.

"Great," Nick lied.

"Sure, tell me all about it." Mac watched Bill Kenny unwrap the bandage and lightly message Nick's leg. Then Kenny poured hot water into a large bucket and Nick gingerly lowered his foot into it.

Jeff Reese opened the door and popped his head in. "Are you in the middle of a powwow or can I come in to chew the fat?" he asked with a grin.

"What powwow?" Mac growled. "This guy never listens anyway. He's all yours."

Jeff gave Mac an affectionate slap on the back as Mac walked out.

"Don't ask me how I feel, buddy," Nick warned with a snarl.

"Who has to ask?" Jeff retorted. "I've seen healthier-looking specimens in the wards of St. Mead's."

"Have you seen Annie?" Nick asked, the snarl gone.

"Barbara's had lunch with her a couple of times. And I ran into her once when I was looking in on Baker."

"How is she?"

"As beautiful as ever." Jeff smiled.

"That's not what I asked you."

"Why don't you go find out for yourself?"

Nick raised a brow. "I've tried, but I guess we both realize this is not the time for hashing things out."

277

"Barbara says she's miserable and is denying it valiantly. I used to think Barb and I had problems, but I think you and Annie are vying for number-one spot."

"Tell me something else."

"Have you told her . . ."

"Try telling Annie Kneeland something when she doesn't want to listen."

"Sounds like someone else I know." Jeff grinned.

"Yeah. Well, maybe that's why whenever the two of us get together fireworks go off. All kinds, if you get my drift."

"I get the picture."

Nick lifted his foot out of the hot water and Jeff handed him a towel, looking down at Nick's ankle.

"What do you think, pal? Can you make it tomorrow?"

Nick looked across at Jeff. "I don't know, Jeff. I sure won't tell you to bet your life savings on me."

"Don't worry. My betting days are over, friend. But I'll be out there in the stands with Barbara and we'll both be rooting for you."

"Thanks, Jeff. It'll feel good to have my own cheering section." Even if the one person he needed the most to be cheering for him wouldn't be there, he thought.

Jeff knew Nick wanted Annie at the match tomorrow and he had been after Barbara all week to get Annie to come with them to the finals. Barbara had asked her a few times, but got nowhere and refused to keep pushing.

Jeff invited Nick to dinner and wasn't surprised when Nick turned down the invitation. "Thanks, Jeff, but tonight nobody deserves my lousy company but me. I need to spend the time figuring out some way to step off the roller coaster tomorrow on two feet."

There was a carnival ambiance at Flushing Meadows. The contrast to Wimbledon was startling. Instead of exquisitely manicured grass courts, the ones at the U.S. Open were skid-marked and well-worn. The largely American crowd, unlike the formally attired English audience, were dressed in all kinds of outlandish costumes. Billboards ringed the area with advertisements for everything from tennis rackets to rye bread. A wafting aroma of hot dogs permeated the air. In the distance the New York skyline was clearly etched on this bright sunny afternoon. The U.S. Open at Flushing Meadows, the site of the 1964 World's Fair, was the total antithesis of the stuffy, affected world of Wimbledon. But as far as professional tennis was concerned, it ranked equal in importance. And to an American it was still the highest accolade, to walk off the New York court a champion.

Jeff was nervously cracking open peanut shells while Barbara, sitting next to him, nibbled on a hot dog. She was as tense as Jeff, waiting for the men's finals to begin. They were also baffled as to what had happened to David. They were

279

supposed to meet him and Marion Baker at the stadium, but the two seats beside them remained empty.

Then about five minutes before the match started, Barbara nudged Jeff and pointed down the aisle. David, trying to maneuver his crutches and cast as he made his way across the row of seats, was being assisted, not by his mother, but by Annie.

Jeff forgot about the peanut shells and Barbara set her hot dog down and gave Annie a big hug.

"Great weather for a tennis match," Annie said with a smile, taking David's crutches while he settled himself into the wooden chair.

"Terrific seats," David exclaimed. They were a few rows from the front, directly facing the net of center court.

Jeff bought David a couple of hot dogs which the boy wolfed down. Annie sat quietly, trying to steady her heartbeat as she watched Nick walk out onto the court.

Nick looked calm and in control, lost inside his own world, oblivious of the spectators, his own aches and pains, the weather—everything but the task at hand.

As the first set opened there was a hush among the packed stands. Nick was first at serve.

The match began disappointingly, neither Nick nor Colliston showing signs of his best form. The pressure showed on them both.

Colliston pulled himself together first, his

shots growing more accurate and aggressive. Nick was surprisingly untempermental. When the linesman made a few questionable calls against him, Nick remained subdued, putting greater concentration on his performance and ignoring the stirrings in the stands.

Annie knew Nick was in pain. She recognized those moves he used to compensate for the pressure to his ankle. The taut, set lines of his face cried out his silent anguish. Annie could feel all his pain and anguish as if it were her own.

Everyone thought the match was as good as over when Colliston took the first two sets handily. The audience appeared convinced that Nick Winters truly was finished. Annie refused to let her mind wander in that direction. She found herself getting increasingly angry at the comments she was beginning to overhear around her about Nick being washed up. David, Jeff, and Barbara were also getting mad.

In the third set, when Nick reared back to wallop a particularly effective serve, the small cheering squad in the fourth row let out a rousing scream. Colliston missed and the squad cheered more vociferously. Nick looked over with a grin. And then he saw her.

Their eyes met across the court and this time there was no question as to what Annie was feeling or thinking. Those sea-blue eyes shone with love, support, and a belief in her man. And Nick's smile left no doubt as to his joy and sense of relief.

It was a stronger man who faced Seth Colliston in that third set—a man who already had sampled a taste of victory. As Nick sliced ball after ball, Colliston began to lose it. The young player who had come out into the field of battle confident of an easy win now started grasping at one strategy after another. He tried fending Nick off with more lobs, but it seemed that no matter what Colliston threw at the former champion, Nick's racket was right there.

When Nick took the third set 6–0, no one was whispering about Winters's being washed up. David was beaming from ear to ear. Jeff looked over at Annie.

"I think we found ourselves one terrific little cheerleader, Dr. Kneeland." He reached across Barbara and gave Annie a loud, smacking kiss.

"That's some partner I got myself," he said proudly. "And if he keeps this up, that Rec Center is going to get the sprucing-up of a lifetime."

"What are you talking about?" Annie stared at Jeff with a baffled expression.

"Hey, don't forget, Reese. Nick promised I get the position of assistant manager," David piped in before Annie's question was answered.

Annie turned from Jeff to David and back to Jeff. "How come I'm always the last to know anything?"

Barbara smiled. "After David's operation Nick and Jeff drew up a partnership contract for the Rec Center. He told us it didn't matter whether he won or lost today—that he'd finally found something he really wanted to do. Half his earnings today are going into building onto the

Center. Nick had a great idea about using the place not only for kids in the neighborhood, but for handicapped children as part of their physical therapy. I think he had a few ideas about a particular orthopedic doctor putting in some of her time, too," Barbara said, her eyes shining.

"Why—why didn't he tell me?" But Annie knew why. She hadn't really given him the chance. Over these past few months they had both gotten into the habit of letting their anger get in the way of real sharing. Annie vowed that was one habit she was determined to break, cold turkey.

It was a new beginning, after all. And a brilliant, glorious ending as well. In the fifth set Nick swept each game. And then came that last, victorious shot. Nick reached far into the rear court and ground the ball backhand with a spinning curve. A stunned Colliston watched the ball hit the ground twice. He never stood a chance of reaching it.

Thunderous shouts and applause broke loose. Nick's eyes shot up toward Annie, who was screaming cheers along with the rest of the crowd. She met his eyes with a brilliant smile and a victory sign. Nick leaped into the air, tossing his racket up and shouting with unrestrained joy. When he landed, he winced for a second as a shooting pain attacked his ankle. But then the feeling passed, and Nick thought, What the hell, I might have a bum ankle, but my head and heart have never been in better shape.

Nick shook hands with a defeated and disappointed Seth Colliston, then he sprinted over the net and ran into Annie's arms. Jeff, Barbara, and David stood close by, still cheering wildly. Nick was handed the winner's trophy. He held it for a moment, then looked deep into Annie's eyes—eyes that promised a love as deep and lasting as time itself. She touched his cheek as he leaned over to kiss her; at the same time he handed the trophy to a beaming David Baker. It was a sweet victory for them all.

LOOK FOR NEXT MONTH'S
CANDLELIGHT ECSTASY SUPREMES ®:

37   ARABIAN NIGHTS, *Heather Graham*
38   ANOTHER DAY OF LOVING, *Rebecca Nunn*
39   TWO OF A KIND, *Lori Copeland*
40   STEAL AWAY, *Candice Adams*

All-new **Candlelight Newsletter**

An exceptional, *free* offer awaits readers of Dell's incomparable Candlelight Ecstasy and Supreme Romances.

Subscribe to our all-new CANDLELIGHT NEWSLETTER and you will receive—at absolutely no cost to you—exciting, exclusive information about today's finest romance novels and novelists. You'll be part of a select group to receive sneak previews of upcoming Candlelight Romances, well in advance of publication.

You'll also go behind the scenes to "meet" our Ecstasy and Supreme authors, learning firsthand where they get their ideas and how they made it to the top. News of author appearances and events will be detailed, as well. And contributions from the Candlelight editor will give you the inside scoop on how she makes her decisions about what to publish—and how *you* can try your hand at writing an Ecstasy or Supreme.

You'll find all this and more in Dell's CANDLELIGHT NEWSLETTER. And best of all, *it costs you nothing*. That's right! It's Dell's way of thanking our loyal Candlelight readers and of adding another dimension to your reading enjoyment.

Just fill out the coupon below, return it to us, and look forward to receiving the first of many CANDLELIGHT NEWS-LETTERS—overflowing with the kind of excitement that only enhances our romances!

Return to: DELL PUBLISHING CO., INC.   B310A
    Candlelight Newsletter • Publicity Department
    245 East 47 Street • New York, N.Y. 10017

Name_____

Address_____

City_____

State_____ Zip_____

Candlelight
Ecstasy Romances™

- [ ] 242 **PRIVATE ACCOUNT,** Cathie Linz 17072-9-16
- [ ] 243 **THE BEST THINGS IN LIFE,** Linda Vail 10494-7-11
- [ ] 244 **SETTLING THE SCORE,** Norma Brader 17660-3-22
- [ ] 245 **TOO GOOD TO BE TRUE,** Alison Tyler 19006-1-13
- [ ] 246 **SECRETS FOR SHARING,** Carol Norris 17614-X-37
- [ ] 247 **WORKING IT OUT,** Julia Howard 19789-9-24
- [ ] 248 **STAR ATTRACTION,** Melanie Catley 18295-6-31
- [ ] 249 **FOR BETTER OR WORSE,** Linda Randall Wisdom 12558-8-10
- [ ] 250 **SUMMER WINE,** Alexis Hill Jordan 18353-7-14
- [ ] 251 **NO LOVE LOST,** Eleanor Woods 16430-3-23
- [ ] 252 **A MATTER OF JUDGMENT,** Emily Elliott 15529-0-35
- [ ] 253 **GOLDEN VOWS,** Karen Whittenburg 13093-X-10
- [ ] 254 **AN EXPERT'S ADVICE,** Joanne Bremer 12397-6-31
- [ ] 255 **A RISK WORTH TAKING,** Jan Stuart 17449-X-20
- [ ] 256 **GAME PLAN,** Sara Jennings 12791-2-25
- [ ] 257 **WITH EACH PASSING HOUR,** Emma Bennett 19741-4-21

$1.95 each

CANDLELIGHT Ecstasy Supreme

- [ ] 29 **DIAMONDS IN THE SKY**, Samantha Hughes..............11899-9-28
- [ ] 30 **EVENTIDE**, Margaret Dobson..............12388-7-24
- [ ] 31 **CAUTION: MAN AT WORK**, Linda Randall Wisdom..............11146-3-37
- [ ] 32 **WHILE THE FIRE RAGES**, Amii Lorin..............19526-8-14
- [ ] 33 **FATEFUL EMBRACE**, Nell Kincaid..............12555-3-13
- [ ] 34 **A DANGEROUS ATTRACTION**, Emily Elliott..............11756-9-12
- [ ] 35 **MAN IN CONTROL**, Alice Morgan..............15179-1-20
- [ ] 36 **PLAYING IT SAFE**, Alison Tyler..............16944-5-30

$2.50 each

At your local bookstore or use this handy coupon for ordering:

DELL READERS SERVICE— Dept. A 107
P.O. BOX 1000, PINE BROOK, N.J. 07058-1000   B310C

Please send me the above title(s). I am enclosing $_____ (please add 75¢ per copy to cover postage and handling.) Send check or money order—no cash or CODs. <u>Please allow up to 8 weeks for shipment.</u>

Name_____

Address_____

City_____ State/Zip_____